D0454516

2018

NO LONGER PROPERTY OF
SEATTLE PUBLIC LIBRARY

PRAISE FOR JENNIFE[R] AND *OUR MAGIC* [HOUR]

Highly Commended, 2017 Victorian Premier's
Literary Award for Fiction

Shortlisted, 2017 NSW Premier's Literary Award for Fiction

Shortlisted, 2014 Victorian Premier's Literary Award
for an Unpublished Manuscript

2016 Staff Pick, *Kill Your Darlings*

Books to Look Out For in December 2016, *A Life In Books*

'All the rapture and calamity of youth, Jennifer Down
is a writer of rare insight and heart.' Carrie Tiffany

'Down's evocation of Audrey's grief is astute, perceptive
and always convincing…It's compelling writing.' *Australian*

'A gritty, evocative story…Unconventional and intimate,
Our Magic Hour is a must-read.' *Canberra Weekly*

'A vivid portrait of our city and its inhabitants.' *Weekly Review*

'An impressive and emotionally sophisticated novel.'
Australian Book Review

'Down's novel is a story about very small things, that all add up
to very big things about grief and friendship, love and death…
Down has an impressive feel for the drama of the ordinary.'
Sydney Morning Herald

'Down has a reserved but beautiful prose…In its maturity and elegance,
Our Magic Hour is a surprising and captivating debut novel. I have no
doubt that Down will produce more quality writing in the future.'
Farrago

'Striking, breathlessly written…Down's clear and confident voice
can play originally with language…An eloquent debut.' *WA Today*

Jennifer Down was born in 1990. She has been published widely, including in the *Age, Saturday Paper, Lifted Brow, Best Australian Stories* and *Blue Mesa Review.*

Jennifer's stories have won several prizes, including the 2014 Elizabeth Jolley Short Story Award and the 2015 Lord Mayor's Creative Writing Award. Her debut novel, *Our Magic Hour,* was highly commended in the 2017 Victorian Premier's Literary Awards and shortlisted in the 2017 NSW Premier's Literary Awards. She was a *Sydney Morning Herald* Young Novelist of the Year in 2017.

jenniferdown.com

PULSE POINTS
STORIES

JENNIFER DOWN

TEXT PUBLISHING MELBOURNE AUSTRALIA

textpublishing.com.au

The Text Publishing Company
Swann House
22 William Street
Melbourne Victoria 3000
Australia

Copyright © Jennifer Down 2017

The moral right of Jennifer Down to be identified as the author of this work has been asserted.

All rights reserved. Without limiting the rights under copyright above, no part of this publication shall be reproduced, stored in or introduced into a retrieval system, or transmitted in any form or by any means (electronic, mechanical, photocopying, recording or otherwise), without the prior permission of both the copyright owner and the publisher of this book.

First published in 2017 by The Text Publishing Company

Cover and page design by Imogen Stubbs
Cover artwork by Luci Everett
Typeset by J&M Typesetting

Printed and bound in Australia by Griffin Press, an accredited ISO/NZS 1401:2004 Environmental Management System printer

National Library of Australia Cataloguing-in-Publication entry
Creator: Down, Jennifer, author.
Title: Pulse Points / by Jennifer Down.
ISBN: 9781925355970 (paperback)
ISBN: 9781925410341 (ebook)
Subjects: Australian fiction. Short stories.

FSC
www.fsc.org
MIX
Paper from
responsible sources
FSC® C009448

This book is printed on paper certified against the Forest Stewardship Council® Standards. Griffin Press holds FSC chain-of-custody certification SGS-COC-005088. FSC promotes environmentally responsible, socially beneficial and economically viable management of the world's forests.

For Roma, Lorna and Fred.

CONTENTS

PULSE POINTS

Ramesh had known Gerry for years—eight, in fact; as long as he and Henry had been together—but this was, in a way, like meeting him all over again.

'This?' he asked, holding up a ceramic figurine of a rabbit, and Henry shook his head. But the water-stained Hopper print in the bathroom was carried lovingly to the sunroom and added to the small pile of things they were taking home with them. Gerry was not his father, of course, and so Ramesh felt no ownership or right to his belongings, or to the decisions about them. He did not understand what was special, which objects were freighted with memory.

Ramesh stopped trying to guess, and started cleaning the place instead. In the end it had been too much for Gerry. The dementia had caused blind spots where he would once have seen weeds in the paddocks, dirt smudges around the light switches. Ramesh filled a bucket with hot water and sugar-soaped every wall in the house, moving methodically from one end to the other. When the water turned grey and tepid, he hauled it outside and tipped it over the grass. Afterwards he felt the flush of satisfaction provoked by manual labour and drying streaks. The place seemed to him lighter.

Gerry's property was four acres of neatly fenced paddocks, proteas, blue gums, melaleucas, banksias, old horse troughs full of stagnant water, two neat pyramids of debris ready for burning off. In the summer months the grass turned dry and pale overnight; in the winter, the air smelled of eucalyptus and turned earth, and the mornings were misty. It felt, perhaps, more rural than it was: Berwick was only a short distance away, and the city itself only forty kilometres or so, but the road to Gerry's house was unmade, and on the hill behind it was the town water tower; a hulking shape crowned with radio masts and transmitters. Henry and his sister, Niamh, had grown up here, though the house was not the same: their childhood home had been razed in the Ash Wednesday fires. This made cleaning out the place at once tragic and unsentimental. The normal artefacts of a childhood had been cremated long ago. What was left was strange: the residue of half a life, a life rebuilt. The photos on the walls were all from the last thirty years. The bedrooms had always been *spare rooms*, empty of Bakelite toys and the desks at which the kids had laboured during their HSC.

Gerry had moved into an aged-care facility, so they were down from Sydney for the weekend to help Niamh get him settled and clear out the house. It was a solemn, tedious task.

Saturday evening they drove to the nursing home and signed the ledger by the front door to confirm they were taking Gerry out for a few hours.

'Niamh's doing a roast,' Ramesh said, trying to distract Gerry where he stood, watching Henry fill the boxes with his neat print: name, time, relationship to resident. The pen was fixed to the table with a cord.

'It's like I'm a bloody parcel,' Gerry said.

'It's like we're signing a guestbook,' Henry said.

'We're kidnapping you,' Ramesh said.

'Good,' Gerry said. 'You can cut me up and dump me in the reservoir instead of bringing me back to this—*prison camp*.'

But in the car Henry jollied him along and he became peaceable, his emotions shifting quickly, like weather systems, the way they did in toddlers. The old man's eyebrows were unkempt. There was a stain on his shirt roughly the shape of the African continent: such indignity in old age! Ramesh thought of his own parents, both still in good health, back in England. The thought of either of them developing the uncertain shuffle of the dementia sufferer made him suddenly, desperately sad. And what about him and Henry, both hurtling towards fifty? Would one of them become the other's carer?

In the front seat, Gerry was telling a story he'd told a million times before and Henry was laughing as though it were new. Ramesh blinked at the dark scrub outside and wished for a swift, lightning-strike death.

Niamh had cut daphne from her garden. The perfume was strong, even with the smell of dinner.

'What's that flower, love?' Gerry asked over and over. 'Your mother used to have it in the driveway.' Niamh's partner Frank sat beside him on the couch and gave the answer again and again, only once sliding a glance sideways at Niamh to grin and roll his eyes.

One of the children crawled onto Gerry's lap and held a stem right under his nose. 'It's *beautiful*,' Gerry said, then sneezed extravagantly. The baby started; the dog ran to the back door. Everyone laughed.

'I'll cut you some to take home, Dad,' Niamh said, wiping her hands on a tea towel. 'We've got loads. It's gone nuts in the last week or so.'

'Don't you call that place my home,' Gerry said savagely. The baby sneezed then, too, and the sound was so different from Gerry's that they all laughed again, and the tension funnelled away.

Ramesh and Henry stood in the kitchen while Niamh tossed the salad. Ramesh folded the serviettes. He was conscious of intruding on the conversation, but he couldn't bear to sit with Gerry. He was sure he'd say the wrong thing, devastate him afresh. Through the doorway he could hear the old man playing a cheerful, repetitive game with the children, and Frank trying to get them all to wash their hands before dinner.

'Does it have to happen so quickly?' Henry said. 'I mean, you and I don't know jack about property, but everyone's saying this is a bad market to sell in.'

'We need money for his bond,' Niamh said. She was talking to the salad, her back to Henry. 'Care's expensive.'

'It's okay. I'm not having a go, Niamhie.'

She glanced at him over her shoulder. 'I did my research,' she said.

'I know you did,' Henry said. He looked surprised.

She put a basket of bread in his hands. 'Here. Can you put this on the table?'

At the home they signed Gerry in again and walked him to his room, but he followed them back down the hallway to the front door. There was an electronic lock with a numbered pad on the wall. Gerry watched as Henry jabbed at the keys and the door slid open.

'What's the code?' he asked huskily.

'Five-five-five,' said Henry, 'two-four-one-hash. I'll come back tomorrow, all right, Dad? Maybe we can go to the Paradise for lunch and watch the footy.'

Gerry followed them to the front gate. It also had a lock. They said goodbye, but when Ramesh and Henry turned back to wave, Gerry was hanging his arms and head over the railing. His hands were flapping, his eyes rolled moronically: he was playing the lunatic, perhaps, or the rabid dog in the cage. Ramesh saw a flash of movement past his shoulder. One of the nursing staff was already heading out to distract him, lead him back to his room.

'Go inside, Dad,' Henry said. 'I'll see you tomorrow.'

In the car the heater sighed. The lights of the little town, the Woolies and the football oval and the houses, disappeared as they rounded a corner, and Henry flicked on the high beams. He drove smoothly, maybe with muscle memory for the road's curves. Ramesh imagined him learning to drive here as a teenager, this long stretch with its guardrail and roadside markers shining in the dark, the trees just blackened shapes.

'He'll get used to it, won't he?' Henry said.

'Of course he will,' Ramesh said. 'It's bloody dreadful, but he's safe where he is. You know he's getting three meals a day and his medication. He can't wander off and get lost anywhere. And it's more company than he's had in a decade.'

Henry was silent. And then he braked hard. Ramesh thought of nothing, bracing for impact, but it didn't come. The car skidded and stopped. He was struck mute, motionless, still unconvinced of the absence of pain, but Henry had unbuckled his seatbelt.

'What are you doing?' Ramesh asked. Henry opened the door and scrambled out. He fell to his knees, got up, and ran to the thing that had made him stop the car, and then Ramesh saw. There was a person lying in the road, face down.

Ramesh stepped out of the car but could not go closer. He could not join Henry where he knelt with two fingers pressed to the body's neck. Ramesh had thought it was a woman, but now he saw it was a small man, thin, in jeans and a hooded jumper. There was blood coming from his ear. It was in his hair.

'Call triple-oh,' Henry said. 'He's got a pulse.' His fingers, bloodied now, were still pressed to the man's neck.

Ramesh fumbled for his phone. He dialled the numbers. First the recording—*You have dialled Emergency triple zero. Your call is being connected*—then the operator, then the dispatcher with a salvo of questions. She was calm, firm. Flat Australian accent.

'What's the address of your emergency?'

'We're on the Beaconsfield-Emerald Road. There's a man— I think he's been hit by a car. He's lying in the road. Please hurry.'

'Can you give me an approximate location?'

'Um—we were driving back from Emerald. Maybe five ks out of Upper Beaconsfield. I don't know, I'm not from the area.'

'Say between Blue Ridge Road and Elephant Rock,' Henry called. Ramesh repeated it.

'What's the phone number you're calling from?'

'Zero-four-one-two,' started Ramesh. Henry's voice sounded distant: *Can you turn off the high beams? They're blinding me.* Ramesh hurried to the driver's side and batted at the lights. For an instant, the world went black. He heard Henry swear.

'Okay. You said you thought this fella had been hit by another vehicle?'

'I don't know. That's what it looks like.'

'Is he conscious?'

'He's not moving. He has a pulse.'

'Is he breathing?'

'Henry, is he breathing? He's—he's breathing.'

'Does he have obvious injuries?'

Ramesh stepped closer. Henry had taken off his jacket and draped it over the man's body. There was a dark slick on the bitumen beneath his head.

'He has a head injury, I think. He's face down.' Ramesh felt his stomach lurch. 'Oh, God. Please hurry.'

'Don't move him around, all right?' the operator said. 'I need you to stay calm.'

'My partner used to be a nurse. He's trying to help.'

'That's good.'

'It's really irregular,' Henry said. Did he mean the man's breathing, or his pulse? The operator had asked something else; Ramesh had missed it. He felt giddy.

'Pardon?'

'I said, is he out of harm's way? You're on the road, is that right?'

'He hasn't been moved. He's in the middle of the road. We've just—we've just stopped our car here so no one will come and—'

'Okay. I want you to put your hazards on. Ask your partner if she thinks he needs CPR.'

He felt a throb of irritation at the careless *she*.

'Henry. Does he need CPR?'

Henry glanced up. 'He's still breathing and he has a weak pulse,' he said. Ramesh repeated the sentence. His inflections were the same; he accidentally mimicked Henry's accent.

'Tell him I want him to start CPR,' said the operator.

'I'm going to put you on speaker,' Ramesh told her. He squatted as close to Henry as he could bear, arm outstretched, phone in his hand.

'I used to be a psych nurse, but not for years,' Henry told the operator.

'All right,' she said. 'We're going to turn him over so he's face

7

up, but really carefully, okay? I need you to stabilise his head and his neck.'

Henry held out his hands as though rehearsing it, then sat back on his heels. His mouth opened and closed. He shook his head.

'Have you done that?' the operator asked. Her voice hung between them, bodiless.

'He's frightened to move him,' Ramesh told her.

'Ask him to use his discretion. If he has experience as a nurse—'

'He's got a bad head injury,' Henry said.

'Okay. We're going to turn him over and start CPR. If he's in this much trouble, and he's not breathing normally, we're not going to do him any more damage. I can talk you through it, okay? You just need to turn him really carefully.'

'Ramesh,' Henry said, 'I need you to help me. We want to keep his body in a straight line while we roll him.' He yanked away the jacket he'd laid over the man. 'I'm going to hold his head up here, and we'll flip him on the count of three. We need to keep his shoulders and neck in the same position.'

Ramesh crouched closer and put one hand on the man's shoulder, the other beneath his hip. The body was a thing still alive: he felt its warmth and substance. They rolled him over on Henry's *three*. Ramesh heard Henry say *Oh my God* in a new, tight voice. The man was a boy, and he had no face: or, his face was a hole. His eyes were shut, and one seemed somehow untouched, but the other, and his mouth and nose, were a pulpy pit of blood and brain and tissue. Ramesh fell backwards. Something surged in his chest. He crawled to edge of the asphalt and vomited into the grass.

'Ramesh,' Henry said. 'Come here. I need you to hold his head.' Ramesh staggered to where Henry knelt, silhouetted in the head-lights. Could he hold the boy's face—what was left of it—without seeing?

'He's not been hit,' he said.

'What's that?' said the operator.

'It's not a hit-and-run. I think he's been shot.'

'Ramesh. Come *here*,' said Henry. 'Grab him behind here and hold his head steady.' He leaned forward, mouth agape over the boy, and froze.

'Henry? Do you remember how to do it?' the operator was asking.

'I can't. He's got blood all over his face. I don't have anything to…' The panic had crept into his voice. He sounded as though he'd been winded. He was still holding his hands in the air like a surgeon might, but they were shaking.

'You can just do chest compressions,' said the operator. 'You don't have to do mouth-to-mouth.'

'Oh shit. Fuck,' Henry gasped. 'He's making a funny noise.'

'It's okay. You're doing a great job. The paramedics are on their way, all right? I just need you to hold it together for a tiny bit longer—'

'I'm doing chest compressions,' Henry said.

'That's good. You're doing so well. Keep going.'

They heard the sirens a long time before the paramedics arrived. Then the splash of light, red and blue on the thick scrub, the dusty roadside, the pale trunks of the eucalypts, the planes of Henry's face. Then the police. The ambulance left and a second police car arrived. They began setting up large floodlights. Ramesh watched Henry talking to one of the officers. He was wrapped in a silver shock blanket, and when he moved it caught the light in a metallic flash. Blood had dried in dark streaks on his cheeks. He was wearing his helpful face to answer questions. It was like watching a stranger. Ramesh was awed and repelled by him. The area where the man had been lying was cordoned off with tape. Ramesh's mobile phone was on the asphalt. He didn't remember putting it down, but he must have. He didn't remember the emergency operator hanging up, but she must have. He lifted the plastic police tape, thinking to retrieve it, but an officer stopped him with a gentle hand to the chest.

'I just need you to stand back here, mate,' he said.

'Sorry—I only wanted—I left my phone there.'

The officer glanced from him to the cordoned-off area. 'That yours?' he asked. Ramesh nodded. The officer looked like he didn't believe him. *Check it*, Ramesh thought. The picture on his screen was of him and Henry on Cradle Mountain, beaming. Deep afternoon light, Henry's head on his shoulder, their fingers locked.

They'd left the kitchen windows open to let out the bleachy smell of cleaning products, and the house was cold. Ramesh made tea the way you were supposed to for someone in shock: black, with three teaspoons of sugar. Henry set out the yellowed crocheted flowers they used for coasters. They sat at the dining table by the wall heater. Ramesh held out his palm, felt the hot dry air.

'There is no way he could have survived,' he said.

'No,' Henry agreed. 'And if he did, he would not be—I mean, there'd be no point.'

'Will you sleep?'

'I'm going to take some of Dad's Valium,' Henry said. 'Maybe you ought to as well.'

The clock on the mantel beat away doggedly. Ramesh looked at Henry's fingers curled around the mug. There were little crescent moons of dried blood in his cuticles. 'I don't think I could do it like that.'

'Do what?' Henry said.

'Shoot myself. I don't know. If I were going to do it, I'd swallow a bottle of pills or jump off a bridge or something.'

Henry stared at him. 'Did you see a gun anywhere near him? He didn't do it to himself.'

He picked up the mugs and teapot and carried them to the kitchen. Ramesh heard the thud of ceramic in the sink, the colicky sound of air in the water pipes. It went quiet again. Henry appeared in the doorway. He was grey around the mouth: for the first time he looked struck with horror.

'I need to wash him off me,' he stammered.

He was so long in the shower that Ramesh began to worry. He stood outside the bathroom listening for the thunk of a shampoo bottle, or the squeak of a heel on the non-slip bathmat. Steam purled from the slit of light where the door met the hall carpet. Once, when they'd only been together a year or so, Henry had got up first thing in the morning to shower. Ramesh was dozing. He knew where Henry had gone; he could hear the water running and his cheerful, sporadic whistle. But half asleep, he'd started to panic. All he wanted was to *see* Henry, to know he was still there. And yet how ridiculous, how pathetic, to stagger into the bathroom, choking for air, terrified, when only ten minutes before Henry's legs had been wrapped around his as they slept. He'd sat on the edge of the bed until he could think clearly again. And Henry had bounded out from the bathroom, naked and joyous, still very much alive and in love with him. Ramesh had never told Henry the story. He'd forgotten it until this very moment, crouched on the nubbly carpet with an ear to the door. At last he went to the kitchen and busied himself with the pantry, which they were halfway through clearing out. There were tins of spaghetti with best-before dates of 1992.

The hot water had almost run out by the time Ramesh got to shower. When he made it to the bedroom, Henry was standing by the window wearing his pyjama bottoms, two fingers pressed to the pulse point on his neck. His bare chest and belly stirred something in Ramesh. He touched Henry's neck with his own fingers, sought the soft hollow by his windpipe. He felt the steady throb. He kissed him there.

The bed was already warm when he turned back the sheets. Henry had switched on the electric blanket for him.

'I feel like we should tell someone what happened,' Ramesh said.

'Who could we tell now?' Henry reached over and snapped off the bedside lamp. 'It's two-thirty.'

Ramesh was used to the sounds of the suburbs. He never noticed barking dogs or level crossings. On the train to work every morning he turned up the volume of his audiobook so it was louder than other passengers' mobile phone conversations. But the country roared. He could hear the air move in the trees. He had grown up in Croydon, moved to Glasgow at seventeen, back to London at twenty-three, then Sydney at thirty-six. As a child he'd stood outside his parents' bedroom listening to his father's whistling snore. He liked living in places where he could hear others alive. He reached for his phone where it sat charging. For an instant he saw his hands illuminated in the bluish light of its screen. He set his rain sound app to the setting called 'Harbour Storm'.

'What are you doing?' Henry croaked. His face was pressed to the pillow. 'You don't need that tonight.'

Ramesh opened his mouth to argue, then he heard the rain outside, like gunfire on the corrugated iron roof.

In the morning they called Niamh to tell her what had happened. *I saw it on the news,* she said. *Was that you two found him?* She began to cry.

In the afternoon they drove to the police station to speak with the homicide detectives. They were interviewed separately, Henry first. Ramesh waited outside on a sculpted plastic chair. He pulled out his phone and scrolled through Facebook, but it felt sacrilegious. He listened to the coppers' laconic conversation. He'd often told Henry, *I don't trust the police*, and meant it. But here, now, these officers reminded him of kids horsing around backstage at a school play.

'Excuse me,' he said at last. 'Is it all right if I go and get the paper?'

They looked up. A young uniformed woman gestured at the door with an open palm. 'You can go and get a coffee if you want, mate,' she said. 'You're not in trouble.'

Afterwards they hurried home so Henry could meet another estate agent. They'd barely stepped in the door when Niamh's old Toyota pulled up outside. She hugged them both tightly. Ramesh felt the bones of her shoulders through her parka.

'How are you feeling?' she asked.

Henry rubbed his face. 'Pretty awful, actually. I can't get it out of my head.'

'I bet you can't.' She stood helplessly, looking from one face to the other. 'You should both see someone. When you get back to Sydney. That's a traumatic thing to happen to a person.'

They moved into the kitchen. The heavy lace curtains had been stripped from the windows to be laundered; the room seemed white and naked. Niamh gave a little *oh* of sorrow when she saw the empty shelves, the fridge bare of pictures and magnets.

'What time's this wanker supposed to be here?' Henry asked.

'The agent? Three-thirty.'

'Hey, while you're here now, do you wanna take a look at the crockery and see what you want?' Henry said. 'I'll take the rest to the op shop tomorrow.'

'I might leave you to it,' said Ramesh. 'Go and visit Gerry.' They both glanced at him in surprise. Their faces were unmistakeably sibling. He felt like crying.

The old man had watery blue eyes. He looked betrayed. Ramesh made two cups of instant coffee in the communal kitchen, half filling Gerry's with tap water so he wouldn't forget it was hot and burn himself. He could get away with certain things, since the old man wasn't his father. They sat in Gerry's room, at the card table and canvas chairs they'd brought from home.

'You understand,' he said to Ramesh. 'You can't take a man's house away from him.'

'I'm sorry, Gerry,' said Ramesh.

'If you're sorry, get me out of here. I'll give over my licence. I'll be good, I promise.'

'It's not about being *good*,' Ramesh said gently.

'Bugger you, then,' said Gerry. 'Bugger the lot of you.'

He turned his face to the wall. Ramesh drew a breath deep into his belly.

'The other night,' he began, 'Henry and I were driving home and we found a man on the side of the road. He was dying, but we didn't know that yet. I didn't even see him till we stopped. Henry just hit the brakes. I thought it might have been a roo.'

Gerry was facing him again, sitting quite still, listening intently.

'We thought he'd been hit by a car, perhaps, or that he was a drunk. I called the ambulance and they told us to start CPR. And we turned him over—he was on his stomach, face down—and half his face was missing. And this woman was on the phone asking Henry to start mouth-to-mouth, and—he barely had a mouth. Somebody had shot him in the head.'

Gerry's face was a rictus of horror.

'His brain was outside his skull,' Ramesh said. 'There was so little for Henry to breathe into.'

A sturdy nurse pushed through the door. An acrid puff of shit and vegetables followed her.

'Hello,' she said when she saw Ramesh, and beamed. 'You're Gerry's son-in-law? He's settling in really well. Aren't you, Gerry? I just came in to see if you were ready for dinner.'

'Is it that time?' said Gerry.

'Roast lamb,' said the nurse.

'I'd better leave you to it, then,' said Ramesh. He walked Gerry to the dining room and sat him at a table with the other patients. He touched Gerry's shoulder and said goodbye. Gerry's eyes flicked over him, to a new anchorless point in space. Ramesh thought of ghosts.

He stopped at the IGA on the way home to buy soup fixings. He hovered in front of the limes. It was the middle of winter and they were expensive. He bought four. They were so small he could hold them in one hand.

It was late afternoon when he got back. The car stirred the dust of the long curving driveway, flattened the dried agapanthus heads that had dropped to the ground. He sniffed his hands. They smelled of skin and oil, his own smell, not blood. He went to the door with a plastic bag in each hand, and Henry opened it before he had a chance to knock. He took Ramesh in his arms, held him fiercely. He kissed his brow.

'I was only visiting Gerry,' Ramesh said. The plastic bags were cutting into his fingers. 'Can I come in?'

'Sorry,' Henry said. He raised his shoulders. 'I worked myself up.' Ramesh waited for him to ask after his father, but he said nothing.

They sat side by side at the kitchen table to peel and cut the vegetables.

'Have you ever had to call an ambulance before?' Ramesh asked.

Henry didn't look up from the leek he was slicing. 'Once, at uni,' he said, 'a friend OD'd at a party and started seizing.' The knife made a rhythmic sound. 'Not really a friend. Just someone I knew. I ended up riding with him to hospital. He was fine. I don't think I saw him again after that.'

Henry carried the chopping board to the stove. The leek hissed when he tipped it into the pot. The groceries were lined up neatly below the window. He picked up one of the small hard limes, held it in his palm as though weighing it.

'What'd you get these for?' he asked.

Ramesh was suddenly shy.

'Mum used to say they were antiseptic,' he said. 'Spiritually, as well as—'

Henry nodded. He put the lime back with the others.

At dusk they walked the perimeter of the property. The grass was silvery in the half-light. They went slowly, without marking rotted fence posts or collapsed sections of wire. They were in their matching boots, bought cheaply at Aussie Disposals a few years back, which Ramesh called *wellies* and Henry called *gummies*. The damp earth softened beneath them.

Henry walked looking at his feet. 'Dad used to tell this story about how after the fires, people whose houses had survived went and laid in the fields to sleep.'

'The trauma was too much for them to return to their homes?'

'He said it was the guilt,' Henry said, 'about still having a bed and a carport when their neighbours' lives had been burned to the ground.'

They'd reached the far end of the paddock, where the ground sloped away.

'It couldn't be totally true,' Ramesh said at last. 'People couldn't have literally slept in the fields, on the ashes. It'd be too hot.'

'Perhaps he meant that they just couldn't return to their beds.'

Ramesh thought of other stories he'd heard—a woman who'd jumped into a dam, thinking water would be safe, and who boiled. Wives walking away from their husbands in the sudden flare of clarity stirred by disaster. The drag of breath through dampened tea towels. The horses screaming. He tried to understand it.

'Henry,' he said. 'I want to go home.'

AOKIGAHARA

I phoned my father when I arrived.

He said, *Your mum's just round at Aunty El's,* in such a way that I knew she wasn't; that she'd left the room with her hand to her mouth when he'd first said, *Hullo, love,* and I felt so sorry for us all.

The hotel room was cool and masculine. I drew back the curtains and looked out. The cityscape glittered from two big windows, like a part of some vast computer. My fingertips tingled if I stood too close to the glass. I wanted to sleep. I got between the starchy sheets. I couldn't hear the city below, but all night I kept waking up and going over to the wide glass panes. I don't know what I expected.

In the morning the view was different and I could see it all as more than a billion lit squares. There was a sprawling park down below. Far off, the symmetrical peak of Mt Fuji. I sat in front of the window, naked, with the glossy map they'd given me in the lobby. I tried to work out where I was.

I met an American woman in the elevator. She was here for work, she said; she visited twice a year. Her husband had long since stopped coming with her.

'He thinks it's exhausting. The sort of place you visit once or twice in your life. He's from Montana.' She gave an apologetic smile. She took out a palm-sized mirror and inspected her mouth. 'Are you here on business?'

'I'm visiting my brother,' I said without thinking. A small mercy: her mobile phone rang, and we smiled at each other as the elevator doors opened into the lobby. I walked away with blood buzzing in my arms. I thought I'd better get my story straight.

In the house I shared with him and Sigrid we'd lain on the living room carpet in an oxy dream. I was too fucked to lift my arms. Tom and Sigrid kissed in a slow, decadent way, faces turned towards each other, but not for long. I dozed there on the floor in a thick shaft of sunlight, my face pressed to the carpet. When a knock came at the door, the three of us were paralysed: Tom gave an indulgent laugh, but nobody moved.

It was all summertime and glory that year: pikelets, braided hair and blood oranges; television, speed, flower crowns, silver dreams, tricks of the light. Long walks home from the city after a night that ended in tears and new jokes and pissing on someone's front lawn, me and Sig giggling with our skirts up around our hips. Power-pedalling up the big hill at night, foreheads spangled with sweat.

We had a poster of the Milky Way, the galaxy of our solar system, tacked up on the wall opposite the toilet, and another poster of constellations beneath it. I learned the names of stars and the pictures they made.

I had no friends. I had only them: Tommy and Sigrid. I was the spectator, the sister; the joyful witness to their Great Passion.

Eri called to say she was running late. I drank a beer and read my book in the greyish light. When she arrived she said *Hisashiburi* and gave me a quick, tight hug. Her hair was cut to her ears. I liked how small and tough she looked.

'I was late at work,' she said. '*Osoku-natte sumimasen.*' She inclined her head and shrugged out of her coat.

I explained what I wanted. Eri might have known. She looked at me levelly while I spoke.

'I can't go with you,' she said. I was the one who looked away. 'But my friend Yui—her father will take you. He's a doctor, but he volunteers there sometimes. You can take a bus to Kawaguchiko station.' Eri took up a pen. She said she'd organise it for me. She wrote the name of her friend and a phone number on a square of paper, and passed it to me with both hands. I never knew when to be humble, when to be reverent. I remembered the set phrases from high school, but not the feel of them in my mouth.

'Thank you,' I said again and again. '*Osewa ni narimasu. Yoroshiku onegaishimasu.*' Thank you for caring for me. Sorry to be a burden. It's what you say. We did it all back-to-front: first there was hardness; afterwards, decorum. We stayed there until after midnight. We talked about our jobs, about our families. Eri lied and said my Japanese was still very good. She was engaged to a school-teacher. She hoped I'd come back for the wedding. I lied and said I would. She reached into her handbag and pulled out a blue envelope. Tucked inside was a photo—she, Tom and I down at Phillip Island, smiling grimly into the wind. Eri wore the pained expression of the exchange student; Tommy grinned from under a ridiculous knitted beanie. He looked healthy, indefatigable, victorious. I was blinking.

Eri leaned by my shoulder, so close that I felt her hair against mine. She looked down at our pale adolescent faces. 'I thought I took more pictures that day, but I could only find this,' she said.

I had the spins at Koenji station. I sobered up on the train back to the hotel. In my room I called Sigrid; lovely Sig who'd stayed with him all that time, who'd weathered his shit when the rest of us could no longer.

'It's all sorted. I'm going the day after tomorrow,' I said. I realised I was going to sob.

'Come home. You don't need to do this for anyone else. You're only doing it for you,' Sigrid said.

'I'm sorry,' I said. 'I'm sorry.'

'What's it like there? Is it cold?'

'You know Buddhists get a new name when they die?' I told her. 'To move away from one world and into the next—the afterlife, or whatever, a dead person gets a new name. So they don't look back.'

'Like Lot's wife.'

I wanted to stick my head into the night, to run around a cricket oval till I was ragged in the lungs. I was aching with a mad, violent energy, but all I could do was curl like a child in the cool bed. When we were kids walking home from school, Mum wouldn't let me cut across the oval without Tom. *It's not good for a little girl to walk there by herself*, she said. I did it anyway, but with a thrumming heart and quick legs, thinking of strange men and bodies in paddocks. It was a much shorter way of getting home. Whenever I banged through the screen door out of breath, schoolbag thumping against the small of my back, Tommy laughed. He'd say, 'What are you *scared* of, Cammy? Worst thing you're gunna see is Jade Pitrowski getting fingered in the tunnel.' He never told Mum. Mostly we walked together.

Dad and I found him once living in a shack up near Marysville. He'd been gone from home a few days. Detective games and phone calls to his friends led us nowhere: we had to wait for Tommy to reach us. He did, at last, and we went to retrieve him. We left Mum standing in the driveway at dusk, telling us to drive safe. I was still in my school uniform. Everyone was frightened of what we'd find this time; what fool's gold lay at the end of the treasure-hunt instructions he'd had Dad scribble down over the phone. In the end, it was a monstrous Tommy, huddled like a dog in his windbreaker and filthy jeans in some abandoned farmhouse. We couldn't go home, he said; we couldn't leave yet. And so we stayed with him in that wormy wood shack. It was not far from the town. Dad drove in on the second morning and bought food and polar-fleece blankets and we tried to make an adventure of it. I was impatient. When it got dark I lit all the candles and sat at the wooden table with my textbooks, highlighting over the words someone else had coloured before me. I learned nothing, remembered nothing. I only did it to say, *Look, you selfish shit, it's not always about you. See what you're doing.* I copied notes into my exercise books with their ruled margins, and did every revision question surrounded by my lumps of molten wax. I remembered nothing.

Dad and Tom went for walks that lasted for hours. I wasn't not invited, but nor was I quite welcome. Once I looked out the window and saw them standing twenty yards apart, knee-deep in grass. Tommy was bellowing something and they were too far away for me to hear at all, but I could see the strain in his neck,

23

his Adam's apple tight and tired, and I imagined him hoarse-voiced. He flung out an arm in a posture of desperation. Dad waited for him to finish.

We stayed there for three days. On the fourth day we drove home, all of us grimy and sour-breathed in our greasy wool jumpers and boots. Me the learner driver up front of the station wagon, easing the car around hairpin bends. Tommy in the back with his headphones, snarling at me to *fucken step on it, will ya*. Dad beside me mouthing to his Buffalo Springfield tape and looking over the sharp, ferny ledges when I wished he'd keep his eyes on the road, or tell me I was taking the corners too fast, because I was afraid. And the asphalt unfurling impossibly before us, canopied by the thickest forest I'd ever seen.

I slept beside a man I'd met in a bar. He was Dutch, an architect, thirty-two, here for a conference. I didn't care. We fucked twice, and afterwards we rolled away from each other and I told him everything. He tried to put his arms around me.

'He was your older brother?'

'Sixteen months older.'

'Almost like twins,' he said. 'I've heard about it, the *jukai*. Sea of trees.'

'I don't know what it will be like,' I said. I felt the grief rising in weak spasms. I got up and went to the bathroom, drank a glass of water from the tap.

'In some ways it's almost a pilgrimage that you're making,' he said pleasantly. His accent made everything sound silly. I wished he'd stop talking. Above the bedhead was a mirrored pane. I could see my own body reflected in it, the shadow of pubic hair, the faint tan lines from a summer ago. White breasts, glass of water in my hand, flesh settled on my hips. There was a smudged handprint on

24

the mirror and I couldn't imagine it had been left by either of us: we'd fucked efficiently, neatly.

I thought I should leave, but he said I should stay. I got back into bed beside him and he reached for me again. He had his arms around me for a long time. One of those blokes who hated silence and loved touching. I wondered if he had a wife or a girlfriend. We must have slept, because I dreamed lightly of flooded fields. I was seeing them from above. I was seeing the water-damaged crops.

We said goodbye in the morning. I got lost trying to find my way back to my hotel. I ended up on the wrong train, then another. I stood on a train platform I didn't recognise, looking at the map with its complicated coloured lines. I might have started to cry, but one of the white-gloved station employees approached. He had a badge of the British flag on his lapel. He asked if I needed help.

'This is Yamanote line,' he said. His fingers traced the map. He showed me where my hotel was, where Tokyo Tower was, where Ginza was, where Akihabara was, smiling the whole time. I kept saying thank you. I felt as helpless as an animal by the roadside. 'Since you are here in Ikebukuro,' the man went on, 'why don't you try the *bōsai-kan?*'

'*Bōsai-kan,*' I repeated dumbly.

'It is a special and interesting earthquake museum. You can experience an earthquake. To feel the feeling.' He held out both gloved hands, fingers splayed, and bent his knees as if bracing himself. '*Wa-a-a-a!*' He laughed. 'Actually, there is information on various type of emergency situations. It is a good attraction. The entry is free of charge. I recommend this place.'

He'd been so helpful that I didn't know how to refuse him. I couldn't simply get back on a train and head off in the right direction. I thanked him over and over again. He gave me a fold-out map, the one I already had three copies of. Marked the route to the museum with a series of neat dashes; warned me it was easy to miss. I kept saying thank you. I wanted to wash the sex off my thighs.

I walked all over the city. I wandered around the streets as if in a hallucination. I was scared if I went back to my hotel I'd fall asleep there in my cool, clean coffin room. I took photos in the fish markets; I bought a small bunch of peonies and carried them around all afternoon like a fool. I walked through the park I kept seeing from my hotel window. In a quiet suburb full of trees I sat in a tiny café styled like a French patisserie. Charles Bradley was playing over the speakers. The coffee was pale and sweet. Ordinarily I would have hated it, but I ordered another and a cake the size of my palm topped with gelatinous fruits and read my book for an hour in the window. It was late afternoon. The light was swimming-pool green. I caught another train, met Eri again for dinner. She brought her fiancé, I wasn't hungry, I was beginning to get nervous. Afterwards the two of them were headed off to sing karaoke with some friends. I turned down their invitation. I had to get up early the next morning.

I sat on the end of the bed to call Dad again. It was neatly made from the day before. I told him about the earthquake museum.

'The Life Safety Learning Centre,' he repeated, and laughed. 'But how did you bloody end up there?' He laughed harder when I told him about the man at the station, uniformed and well-intentioned, and how I'd gone out of politeness. I told him about the earthquake simulator.

'It was frightening,' I said. 'It went on for longer than I expected. I was surprised.'

He asked if I wanted to speak to Mum. I said I had to get up early the next morning.

• • •

There was a car accident. It wasn't me driving round the Black Spur, it was Tommy dozing off in the car on Swan Street, me in the passenger seat reaching over to grab at the wheel. He ruptured his spleen and in hospital he got high on pethidine. He had a vision—colour and dreams in his arms—and all I got was to sit by his chair. He went off the SSRIs after that. We learned about them when I did my psych rotation, their uses and side effects. Of course that doesn't happen to everyone. Of course if you feel drowsy or otherwise affected, you shouldn't drive. Of course. He went cold turkey, like you're not supposed to.

'What does it feel like?' I'd heard Sigrid ask him once. One of the afternoons when we'd cycled around the Merri Creek Trail with bottles of Mercury tinking in our crates, sprawled out in the sun, read to one another, done the quiz in the paper. We had so much time.

'Dizzy,' Tommy had said, 'these sort of—electric-feeling brain zaps. Like shivers in your head that roll through.' He'd pressed his hands to her hair, scrunched his fingers, raked them down her skull to her neck, but tenderly. Sig's shoulders tensed. They'd thought I was asleep. I realised it was too late to let them know I was listening. 'Like looking through fog. I just feel out of it.'

'Must be dreadful,' she'd said.

'Gunna be good when it's over,' he'd said. My brother with his silly, lovely grin, withdrawing from the good pills. That was May. He went to Japan in September. We'd all waved goodbye to him at the airport. He'd swaggered off singing 'The Internationale' for reasons I've long forgotten, waving his windcheater at us till he disappeared through the silver doors. The security guard had laughed and dad had laughed and Sig laughed, too, but she'd been crying. Her eyes were leaking and she was doing that ragged breathing. I thought she was just getting ready to miss him. In a way she was. Maybe she'd known something then that the rest of us hadn't.

I'd brought a book to read on the bus but I ended up with my face to the window the whole way. I slipped in and out of light sleep, tiny flickering dreams. A sign in a window I couldn't read; tunnels into the earth; my father with white smoke rising from his belly or chest, he was on fire and didn't realise. I woke with a start and looked around me. I wondered if I'd cried out. I kept my headphones on and looked out at the mountain drawing closer.

Mr Ukai met me at the bus stop. He was a small, slim man. He wore a parka. He held out his hand for me to shake.

In the car he played Bob Dylan.

'*Osewa ni narimasu.* Thank you for doing this,' I said.

'It's good to be able to help. I go there to help anyway.' His English was clear. His eyes did not move from the road.

'Even so. It's a big ask—it's a big favour. I'm grateful. *Yoroshiku onegai itashimasu.*'

'*Ii-i-e.* I think it is not so good for you to go there by yourself,' he said gently. 'I think, if you are not too tired, we will go to there now. We don't want to be in the forest after dusk. It is a dense place.'

'I've read a little bit about it,' I said. 'I read about that book. *Kanzen jisatsu manyuaru.*'

'*The Complete Manual of Suicide.*' He shook his head. 'I think it is maybe a hysteria. I think you cannot blame a book. This sadness is an epidemic. It did not come from bookstores. But—' we slowed at a corner and he turned to look at me, one hand on the gear-stick—'I have not read this book, so maybe I don't know.'

The roads were wet. The trees were fat with the sort of haze I imagined would burn off later in the day. I felt as if I'd been awake for a long time, but it was still morning.

'Yui tells me you are medical student. Very good.'

'Well, I'm not very good. I'm just passing,' I said. 'And I still don't know if it's what I want to do.'

'I still don't know, either. And I am a doctor for thirty years.' He laughed. 'What do you like most?'

'I want to be a diagnostician. I like solving puzzles,' I said. 'But I don't know if I work hard enough for that.'

We pulled in to a car park. We'd arrived suddenly. I hadn't been looking for signs. Mr Ukai sat for a moment after he cut the ignition, looking at something I couldn't see in the rear-view mirror. I thought he was going to ask me if I was ready, but he just reached into the back seat for his plastic water canteen.

From the car boot he took out a smaller rain jacket and handed it to me. He retrieved a backpack, a torch and a length of fluorescent-yellow nylon cord, neatly coiled. That nearly brought me to my knees. I had a bad feeling in the guts. It smelled like new earth out here, petrichor; like bright air. I tried to think about that instead of the nylon cord.

Mr Ukai shut the boot gently. He slung the backpack over his shoulder, and his waterproof jacket gave out a rustle.

'*Ja, ikōka?*'

We started towards the entrance. The leaves were wet underfoot.

'People say it's a mystical place, they say, *nanka*, many kind of thing, but it's just a forest,' he said. 'The mystery is why are so many people sad.'

It struck me as a distinctly un-Japanese thing to say. The woods were darker than I'd imagined. It was all electric green moss and untamed tree roots crawling over the forest floor. It felt prehistoric. We came to a length of yellow rope stretched across the path. There was a sign that said *No Entry*. Mr Ukai stepped right over it, then held it down so I could do the same.

'I think it is best, from here, if I walk first,' he said. He inclined his head. I nodded.

'Of course.'

'Cammy-san. If the experience becomes too heavy, *nanka, tsurai*—we will go back to my car. Please do not be troubled. Do—not—hesitate.'

He pronounced my name *kami*, like 'god'. I nodded again. I had my thumbs looped through the straps of my backpack. I felt like a child on an excursion.

We fell into step single-file, me behind him. I wondered what he'd meant, exactly, with his polite broken English. There was such a chasm between us. I thought about Eri saying *I can't go with you.*

I kept my eyes fixed on Mr Ukai's back, or on my own running shoes, caked with wet leaves. When he started humming to himself, I thought it must have been safe to look up. There was tape everywhere, strung between trees. Some of the trunks had numbers spray-painted on them. Mr Ukai stepped off the main trail onto a smaller one. He looked back at me. He said, '*Daijōbu?*' and I said, '*Daijōbu.*' I could feel sweat cooling on my neck.

It had been weeks before we'd had the funeral. There were complications bringing Tommy's body back. For a while the Japanese seemed to think there should be an autopsy, and that they should be the ones to undertake it, but that faded. I had half a Valium before the service and another after I'd read my eulogy.

There was no word for *closure* in common Japanese. I'd looked it up online in my hotel room the other night.

Mr Ukai had stopped humming. He was walking respectfully. Everything he did was gentle. He looked around openly, scanning the forest, where I dreaded it.

There was human detritus everywhere. Plastic umbrellas, food wrappers, mittens, lengths of rope, a bicycle, a pair of scissors, a blue tarpaulin. The trees were so thick overhead, I wondered how they let any light through. I could see why Tommy would have loved it here.

Mr Ukai paused. He waited until I was beside him, then he pointed at the base of a tree a little way off the path. There was a marker at its base. Someone had left a bouquet of flowers, pink cellophane, and a tiny banquet of food, laid out on a piece of cloth.

'It is recent,' Mr Ukai said. 'Maybe someone else is making our same journey today.'

A few steps further I saw a skull turned green and a rotten shoe. There was a crop of tiny mushrooms growing by the heel of the shoe. Their stalks were young and firm. I squatted with one hand on a damp tree and vomited. Mr Ukai handed me a pocket pack of tissues. I wiped my mouth. I waited until I was sure I wasn't going to do it again, then I stepped past Mr Ukai. I zipped my water canteen back into my backpack. I apologised in a way that sounded too formal.

'Maybe a place near here would be good,' he suggested when we started walking again.

'It's beautiful, but there's no light.'

'Aokigahara is a very dense place. That's why it is *jukai*. Sea of trees.'

'I know,' I said. I felt rude. 'I just thought maybe we could find a clearing.'

We walked for a long time. I watched the soil under my feet. The trees closed over almost completely, so that I had to bend my head in parts, but we did come to a clearing.

'Here,' I said, 'I think this is a good place.'

'It is,' he agreed.

My mouth tasted like vomit. I took off my backpack and fished out the plastic bag.

'Cammy-san. If you wish, I can go somewhere else. So you can be discreet.'

I looked up at him. I shook my head. 'I don't need to be here long.'

I took the letters and the hammer out of the plastic bag. I chose a tree. I lined up the pieces of paper. They were neatly folded into four, no envelopes. I fixed them to the tree. The nails were probably too small, but they held. I nailed Eri's Phillip Island photo to the trunk, too, then the yellowed poster from our bathroom in the Yarraville house, the one with the constellations.

When I finished hammering I stood back to look at my shrine. Mr Ukai was on the other side of the clearing, sitting on the trunk of an enormous fallen tree. He was watching me with a placid face.

'Please take your time. Do not hurry,' he said.

'I think I'm done,' I said. I left the hammer by the tree. I had no more use for it.

Afterwards Mr Ukai took me back to his house. His wife served us green tea and small sweet cakes and mandarines with tough skins. We sat at a low table. Mr Ukai said it was all right not to kneel. Mrs Ukai looked at me the way you might look at an orphan. She asked gentle questions. We winced at each other.

Their daughter Yui was my age. She arrived home from university and introduced herself.

'Yui has just been on student exchange. For one year. In Austin,' Mr Ukai said.

'Texas,' Yui said. She gave a little smile. Fathers and daughters were the same everywhere you went. Mrs Ukai insisted on cooking me dinner. She made yudofu, tsumire and daikon. I was surprised at how hungry I was.

'Yudofu is my favourite,' Mr Ukai said. 'I have tried to cook yudofu myself, but I am not so good as my wife.' He laughed pleasantly. His wife did not speak English. She smiled at me through the steam rising from her bowl.

After dinner Yui and I stood in the dark outside on the wooden verandah and smoked a joint. She spoke with an American accent so convincing she even had a slight drawl.

'I'm sorry about your brother.'

'It's okay. I don't think there's anything we could have done to stop him.' My arms were feeling warm on the inside. I had the sudden urge to stand close to Yui, to let our arms touch, to see if hers were hot, too, but some part of me realised I was high.

'Why did he come here to do it?' she asked.

'I don't know. He did a student exchange here when he was in high school. He never knew what he wanted to do. I'd never heard him talk about Aokigahara before. But now I've seen it, it makes sense to me.'

'It's a beautiful place,' Yui said. I wanted my mother.

The last bus to Tokyo left at 8.10 p.m. Mr Ukai drove me back to Kawaguchiko station. As we approached the station I began to thank him again, clumsily. We parked beneath a floodlight.

'There is a Japanese saying—*Nodo mo to sugireba atsusa o wasureru.* Do you understand?' Mr Ukai asked. I shook my head. 'It means "One forgets the heat once it has passed down the throat."'

My backpack was heavy on my lap. I went on thanking him. He got out and waited until I was on the bus. I waved at him from the window. He was still standing there when the bus pulled away. I waved until I couldn't see him anymore.

I felt as if I'd been gone for days when I got back to the city. I couldn't bear the trains and the streets. I couldn't bear this country.

I felt filthy. I started to undress to get in the shower, and then I thought I'd better phone my dad if I was going to do it at all.

'I went. I saw it.'

'Oh, Cammy,' he said. 'Are you all right?'

I sat on the edge of the bed.

'Do you remember that time we went to get Tommy from the mountains, and we drove home through the Black Spur? The trees were thicker than that.'

He began to cry. I heard him sucking in air through his teeth.

WE GOT USED TO HERE FAST

1996

In the morning we walk all the way to the beach to count puffer fish. Me five, her four, plus a dead rat. Lally crouches and pokes it with a stick. There are maggots squirming in there and it makes me feel crook. It's the second day of school holidays. It's not raining, but it's so cold the air feels wet. Lally picks up twigs and holds them like cigarettes. Her breath comes out in clouds. I can tell she's trying to be grown-up but she looks constipated. We walk all morning, up and down the creek, then to the train station, because that's where it's safe to cross the freeway. By the time we get to the Snakepit, the footy's started. Lally's tired, which is sort of Mum's fault since she's the reason we had to stay out of the house. At half-time we find the sausage sizzle. The guy's wearing a Karingal guernsey but he's nice. He asks if we want a sausage each, and when I tell him I've only got sixty cents he gives us two anyway.

The spare key's been moved from under the mat at home. Lally whispers, *Knock, Sam,* and I say, *Fuckoff will you, Lally.* We go around the back and I try to do the security door quietly. But inside the washing machine's banging against the wall, and there's a smell I can't work out, like cooking. I realise I never checked if there was a weird car out the front. I get the maggoty feeling inside me. Lally's starfish hand grabs a fistful of my T-shirt. We move towards the kitchen like we're chained together.

I don't recognise Nan at first. It's been a long time since I've seen her. She's wearing shorts. Her legs are like two brown sticks, speckled and skinny.

'I thought you two had run away,' she says, and holds out her arms for a hug. I want to ask what she's doing here but I don't in case that's rude. Lally's eyes are moving from me to Nan. Finally she says, 'Where's Mum?'

'She's in bed. I thought we'd have some lunch, then we'll go and get some shopping done. Then we're going to pack. You two are coming with me for a bit. Come up and visit Granddad.'

'Do we have to go?' Lally asks.

'Yes,' Nan says. 'But it's gunna be a good time. We'll make an adventure.'

The next morning she wakes us so early the birds aren't even up. Lally's dead weight. Nan has to tug her arms into her wind-cheater, shove her feet into her sneakers. There's all dust and hair and grot in the Velcro straps and it makes my tummy swim. We kiss Mum goodbye. She's even sleepier than Lal, but she stands in the doorway to wave us off, pulling her dressing-gown cord tight. Her teeth are chattering so loud I can hear them.

In the car Lally falls asleep again straight away, mouth open. Puffer fish. Once in a while a snore catches in her throat, and Nan and I do little smiles at each other. Then I fall asleep, too. When I wake up there's a bit of dribble crusted at the corner of my mouth and I hope Nan hasn't seen. It's just getting day. There are light streaks in the sky. The clock says 6.46. We pull into a McDonald's. Lally wakes up when the car stops, says, *Where are we.* Nan says, *I'll show you.* Inside we get a whole serve of pancakes each. I finish Lally's and then we pretend the empty white containers are UFOs. Nan spreads out a map on the table.

'We'll see how we go today,' she says. 'Maybe we'll get to Dubbo. Maybe Coonabarabran.' We're going all the way to Toowoomba. Her fingernails are the colour of clam shells.

'Where are we now?'

'Shepparton. See, near the border of New South Wales.'

We've never been out of Victoria. I can tell Lally doesn't get it. There are lots of things I know and she doesn't, since I'm four years older.

The car trip takes forever. I move to the backseat. Me and Lally play that game where you make up a story by saying a word each at a time.

'Once.'

'There.'

'Was.'

'A.'

'Ugly.'

'Very.'

'Lally, that doesn't make sense.'

'It does if you say *little* next. Once there was a ugly, very little...' She starts cackling again.

'You'll lay an egg,' Nan says.

When the stories get too rude, we lower our voices until we're whispering, and then we're not even joining our words to make a story anymore, just saying the worst ones we can think of. Pissbuggerbumshitdickarseweebastardfuck. I know the real worst word, but I don't say it. That's another thing Lally doesn't know.

We drive all day. I've never been in a car for this long. I reckon even Nan's got the wriggles, because she starts saying, *Not much longer*. I sleep. When I wake up we're pulling into a car park in front of a giant satellite dish. Lally's sitting with her face pressed to the window.

'What is it?' she asks. 'Sam? Is that a spaceship?'

'It's a satellite,' I say, even though I've never seen one that huge so I might be wrong.

'It's a radio telescope,' Nan says. 'When they first walked on the moon, we all watched it on telly. And this station was the one with the signal that went out to the whole world. Even America.'

The place is empty. There's a visitors centre with a café, plastic chairs and striped umbrellas, but it's all packed up for the day. Out the front are two smaller satellite dishes, both white, facing each other. They're far apart, maybe the length of the school oval.

'If you go and stand in front of one, Sam,' Nan says, 'and Lally, you stand in front of the other, and you whisper into the middle of the dish, you'll be able to hear each other.'

I don't believe her, and I can tell Lally doesn't, either. Nan just smiles. 'True,' she says. 'Gotta whisper, though.'

Lally looks from me to Nan, then trots off. I head for the other dish, feeling dumb. I lean in close.

'Hi, Sam,' I hear her say.

'Hi,' I whisper back.

'I can hear you,' she says. It sounds like she's right in my ear. I turn around to look. She's standing in her purple tracksuit facing the other dish. Her hands are cupped like she's telling it a secret.

'Can you hear me, Sam?'

'Yes.'

'Do you think Mum's sad because we left her?'

'No, Lal.'

'When do you think we'll go home?'

'I don't know.'

'Do you think she knows where we are?'

'I don't know.'

'Do you think she misses us?'

'Yes.'

I glance over my shoulder. Nan's waiting with her arms crossed, but in a nice way, like we've got time.

We keep driving to Dubbo. It's dark when we get there. We've been in the car the whole day. I ask if we're gunna sleep in the car and Nan says no. We drive around some more looking for a motel. There's no room at the first two. 'Like the story of the baby Jesus,' Lally says, and Nan laughs. 'You'll lay an egg,' Lally dares, and I tell her not to be cheeky but Nan just keeps laughing until she's wheezing. We find a motel. There's a paper strip across the toilet seat. I crack Lally up by pretending it's a present wrapped up for me. We go for tea at a Chinese restaurant with thick red carpet. Walking back to the motel we stop at a payphone so Nan can call Granddad. Lally's pretending to smoke again, cloudy breath. I'm hopping from foot to foot. Nan doesn't seem to feel the cold at all. The orange phone booth light hangs over her.

In the dark, later, Lally says my name. 'Do you think we could make them dishes?' she asks. For a second I think she's talking about the beef and black bean we had for tea.

'What are you talking about, you whacker?'

'The whispering satellites.'

'Go to sleep, Lal, chrissake.'

'If we could make that in our house,' she says, 'we could talk without Mum being angry.'

When it's Easter I'm twelve and Lally's eight, and we've been in Toowoomba for almost a year. Lally pissed the bed every night for three weeks, but Nan never got angry once. I think I'm meant to remember Mum's face but it's sort of swirly in my head. We got used to here fast. We got used to Granddad, with his menthols and radio and pill pack that the pharmacy girl drops in every week. His funny sayings like *colder than a frog's fart*. He teased Nan about believing in baby Jesus until Lally announced she believes in baby Jesus, too. He took us to the pet shop in town and bought us a guinea pig. We did a vote and named him Harry. Granddad loves shows and stories about mysteries, but not the sort police detectives can solve. His favourite mystery is about two guys who died on a hill in a jungle in Brazil. No one knew how they died but they were found wearing raincoats and eye masks, like what rich ladies wear to bed in the movies, only made out of lead. One of them also had a note that read: *16.30 be at the determined place. 18.30 swallow capsules, after effect protect metals wait for mask signal*. That's the part that really gets Granddad going.

It's April when the phone calls begin. Mum starts wanting to speak to me and Lally. It feels sad, like she's left out, so I try to make it sound like things are boring. It's sort of true, but I like it. The weeks have a regular heartbeat. Tuesdays we go to the RSL because it's eight-dollar seniors' meals, then Nan plays the pokies. Thursday's pension day, which is groceries then fish and chips. Friday's swimming practice.

Lally and I are playing Power Rangers in the backyard. It's her favourite game but I hardly ever play it with her because I'm embarrassed. Granddad says, *Mum's on the phone* and we ignore him for a bit but then we go in. Straightaway Mum's voice sounds different, like she's swallowed some colour. She asks heaps of questions. It reminds me of when she was in love with Gary and she laughed all the time. She says, *How about if I come up to visit.* Nan and Granddad are smiling at me and Lally's going, *What, what Sam, what's she saying.* I don't know why, but my guts go sicky. I talk a bit more, then I push the phone at Lally. I lock myself in the old outdoor toilet. Bad watery shit comes out of me and I know it's because I'm guilty about not wanting Mum to come.

After tea Nan and Granddad tell us we can play in the backyard a bit longer, but Lally and I squat on the bricks under the kitchen window so we can hear them talking inside. It smells like rain even though a storm hasn't come yet. Nan and Granddad are talking back and forth, but not in a way of arguing. They keep saying *She* and I can't work out if they mean Mum or Lally or someone else. They keep saying *Custardy.* The crickets are so loud it's hard to hear much else.

'What's custardy,' I say, even though it's not like Lally would know. But she puts a finger to her lips.

'It's who owns the kids,' she whispers.

'How do you know that?'

She shrugs. It pisses me off, the way she knows something I don't, the bored way she explains it. I'm suddenly so mad that my body can't hold it in. I reach out and shove Lally hard. She flies backwards and lands on her bum on the bricks. Her head hits the corner of the card table. She scrunches her eyes closed. I wait for her to cry, but she doesn't make a noise. The floodlight flicks on and Granddad's in the doorway.

'Come on, it's dark. Jump in the bath, Lal.'

She trails inside after him. Doesn't look back.

• • •

41

We walk home from school trying to solve the mystery of the lead mask men. Lally reckons the masks were like sleeping masks, only magic, and instead of putting the men to sleep, they sent their souls somewhere else, like heaven maybe, except their bodies got left behind. We're crossing under the rail bridge, almost at the big park on O'Quinn Street, about to cut across the grass when I feel a tap on my shoulder. Tegan Foster's standing there with her little sister, who's younger than Lally. She says *Hey* and I say *Hey* back even though I just saw her at school. Her bag hook's near mine.

'What are you guys talking about?' she asks. Lally starts telling her the whole story. Sometimes I have to interrupt because she leaves out important bits. I feel dumb, though, and when Tegan looks at me it feels like my face is shrinking. She's standing with her hand on her hip. I wait for her to laugh, but she just says, *Maybe they were time travellers, and the pills sent them*—she waves her hand. The four of us stand there. Tegan's sister says, *Are we going?* and Tegan says, *You guys go and play on the playground.* Lally looks dubiously at the patch of tanbark, but the two of them take off running, schoolbags jumping up and down on their shoulders.

Tegan says, *C'mere*, and starts walking back towards school, towards the low rail bridge. I'm following her brown ponytail, blue scrunchie, past the beams painted red and white stripes, past the sign that says LOW CLEARANCE 2.6M, through the broken bit of the wire fence, up the muddy rise over the stones and pieces of glass and dirt until we're right underneath the train tracks. We both have to crouch. I can feel the sweat pricking the behinds of my knees. Then she kisses me. It's sort of a surprise but sort of not. Her mouth is warm and I hope I'm doing it right. I keep my eyes closed so I can concentrate. She says, *Open your teeth, dummy*, and I unclench my mouth a bit, and her tongue goes in. I'm holding both Tegan's hands. I don't remember grabbing them. It feels like an earthquake's

42

coming, but then I realise it's only a train going over us. We stop kissing to listen. This close, it sounds like the end of the world. Suddenly Lally's standing down below, near the hole in the fence.

'That playground's shit,' she says. Tegan laughs and drops my hands. She says, 'Where's Jadie?' We crab-crawl back down the slope and walk back towards the park. Tegan's sister is waiting by the dunny block with its painted mural. After that, Tegan and I hold hands sometimes at school when we line up for assembly. Some days after school we go to sit in the concrete pipes to kiss. Lally knows she's not invited.

We have a working bee to get ready for Mum. Granddad shows me how to mow the lawn. We're out the front doing the edges when Nan starts yelling. We both run, but I'm fastest, and when I get to the backyard I see her holding Lally by the shoulders and she's screaming, *What have you done, what have you done.* She's shaking Lally so hard that Lal's head is bobbing on the stalk of her neck. I look to see if Lally's peed but she hasn't. Nan's the one who's upset. Lal just looks bored.

'Stop, Shirl. What happened?' Granddad says. And that's when I see Harry the guinea pig in the fresh-cut grass by Lally's feet. Dead.

Nan lets go Lally's shoulders. 'She had it like this'—she's speaking to Granddad, holding her hands like there's a sandwich in them—'and she squeezed it till it died. She looked right at me.' Her voice is high and rattly. Lally bursts into tears. They're terrible sobs that come up out of her legs.

'All right,' Granddad says. 'I'm sure it was an accident. It's all right.'

In that second I see Nan decide it was an accident, too. She takes Lally into her arms. Later Granddad and I put Harry in a tissue box and bury him under the hibiscus.

School breaks up on Friday. On Saturday Mum arrives and says she's taking us back to Melbourne.

2016

The day Sam was discharged, we waited all morning for the specialist to come in, then the surgeon, then we waited for the paperwork. No one seemed to know what was going on. Lunch. He was supposed to be gone by then. I had to argue until he got a meal. He had a spoonful of mashed potato and pushed the rest away. A shift change. I waited by the nurses' station, ready for a fight. He stood beside me. He leaned against the wall. His face was pinched and grey.

I was so full of rage that I didn't notice him fading. When I turned he was sitting in a plastic chair by the elevator, barely upright. His earlobes poked out from his woollen hat.

Outside he ripped the plastic band from his wrist. He wanted to go to his ex-boyfriend's house. They'd been separated for six months by then, but they were still close. He phoned a cab.

'At least let me come with you,' I pleaded with him. 'Theo would hate to see you pull up in a taxi by yourself. Just wait five minutes and let me call work.'

'I've waited all fucken morning. And I want to go by myself.'

'Will you please do this one thing for me.'

'I just want to go,' he said.

The taxi arrived. I put his bag on the seat beside him, tugged his beanie down to cover his ears. He was crabbed like a frightened child. He weighed fifty-eight kilos.

At home I moved from room to room. I kneeled beside my bed and thought about saying a prayer, but I wasn't sure what to ask for. I called Sam. It went straight to voicemail. *Just making sure you*

44

got to Theo's okay, I said. *Text me YES when you can.*

There aren't many photos of us as kids. A few of Sam as a baby, another series from when I was born. Then a big gap, like we didn't exist for a while. There are a few pictures from the year or so we spent living up north with Nan and Granddad. Nan had a little compact camera. I remember the mechanical buzz it made when you slid the front part open. She used to give me her empty film canisters to keep stuff in—sequins and tiny pebbles, apple seeds, knock-off Polly Pocket dolls and accessories that Nan bought me, which I never played with because I thought they were naff, but couldn't bear to throw out.

My favourite photo from then was taken when we went on holidays to Tewantin. There was this weird, dusty old bottle museum, a house full of old glassware and beer paraphernalia, and in the yard was a big bottle two storeys high, constructed from old glass stubbies. You could walk around inside it and climb a winding stairwell to the top, where a metal slide curled around the exterior of the thing. They gave you hessian potato sacks to sit on so you'd go really fast. I remember being scared but not wanting to let on to Sam. Somehow Granddad knew, and he made it seem like he wanted to have a go. He climbed to the top with us, and we watched Sam shoot down the warm metal. Then Granddad got on the sack and sat me between his knees, and we slid together. We must have done it dozens of times—me by myself, eventually, and Granddad, too, like a big kid, over and over. I remember his knees being sore by the end of it from climbing the stairs. Even Sam didn't get sick of it. Inside the big bottle it smelled earthy. The air was yellow through the glass, swimming with dust. At one point all three of us squished onto the same hessian sack and slid down together, and Nan got a picture. Granddad's at the back with his arms in the air, mouth agape, like he's on a roller coaster. Sam's in the middle, with one arm around me. He's laughing. He was always such a serious kid that it's almost a shock to see. He's not worried, or playing it cool, or pretending he's too old for slides. And there's me in front. I'm missing my two front teeth, which you can see because my mouth's wide open, eyes shut tight like I'm really cackling—*You'll lay an egg*, Nan used to say—and my hair's a dirty blonde bowl cut, stringy fringe, wonky off-centre part.

You wouldn't recognise either of us now if you saw that photo. My hair darkened as I got older; puberty gave my face a new hard shape. Sam looks like a young man dying of blood cancer. So I don't recognise us in the picture, but I like having proof of that day: the blinding joy, the thrill of the hot winding metal, our tangled arms. I try to remember that version of my brother.

We were lucky to have that time. Toast soldiers, talkback radio in the morning, Granddad with his unsolved mysteries about lead masks and Harold Holt and the nine ski hikers who died inexplicably on a mountain in Russia. Nan cleaned the dirt from my bellybutton and behind my ears with tea tree oil and said *Oh, you grot!* but always in a nice way. Nan and Granddad tried to make everything as normal as they could, like they were our parents, just old. It didn't end because I killed Harry the guinea pig, but that happened right before Mum reappeared and took us home to Melbourne, so for a long time, in my head at least, those two things were linked. Cause and effect. I was maybe fourteen when I told a psychologist about it—I'd been seeing her because of something that had happened in resi, but for some reason Harry popped into my head. I was so ashamed to tell her, I wept. She was nice about it, though. She said something about how when I was that age, I'd never had much control over anything that happened to me, and how I probably wanted to know what it was like to be the one in charge.

I don't know why I did it. I only remember Sam's face, the

revulsion on it, and how I could fool Granddad, but not him, that it was an accident.

He was back in the hospital four days later, worse than before. He had two transfusions in a week. I called Theo, who came straight-away. He sat on the end of the bed.

'When I didn't hear from you after the other night,' he said, 'I got worried you'd gone off to die by yourself like a dog.'

'You've got no idea what it's like,' Sam said.

'I think I've got a bit of an idea. Fuck you.'

'You don't. What if I want to be by myself? No one's asking me what I want. They just keep giving me clean blood.' He was short of breath. Grey lips.

They had a fight right there in the room. I kept trying to leave but they both wanted me to witness it. We all cried. Theo left.

Sam asked what the weather was like outside. I told him it was pissing down.

'Remember when we got stuck in that motel room in Coffs Harbour during the floods?' I said.

'Mm,' he said.

'And then bananas got really expensive.'

'All the sugarcane was fucked.'

'That was coming down, with Mum,' I said. 'Remember on the drive up with Nan when we stayed at the Peter Allen motel in Tenterfield?

'She had the tape of him. She played it in the car.'

'Remember when she came to get us? She was wearing that jacket. Hot pink, made out of, like, parachute material.'

'I just remember her shorts. Middle of winter.'

'We stopped at the whispering dishes at that CSIRO place,' I said.

'I don't want to speak about it anymore,' he said.

I hated being split up, but that's what happens to *sibling groups*. That's what we were called. No one takes you in twos. Nan and Granddad would have, but by then Nan was wandering at dusk and forgetting to eat, and Granddad couldn't look after three of us.

Sam was at the age where they try to transition you out of resi and into independent living. They put him up in a motel room. I got to visit him once. The caseworker left us alone, at least. Sam made us instant coffee with powdered milk. It made my heart go too fast. He'd stopped going to school by then. He said he felt like he was in jail. He asked me how I was going. I wanted to make him hurt, so I told him about how a boy tried to fuck me with a longneck. He got so angry I thought he was going to tear himself apart. He raved and shouted, searching the room for something to destroy. But he caught himself, stilled himself in time. I saw him working to contain himself, to flatten his rage.

That was not long before he got sick the first time. I've never seen him look as mighty since. He thinks I never forgave him for what happened but it's not true. I know he couldn't have helped it.

That last night in the hospital I came straight from work. Theo had already left. It was dark out.

'The oncologist was supposed to come again at eight,' Sam said, 'but I don't think he's coming now.'

'I don't think he's coming, either,' I said. I went to stand by the window. Outside, below, the suburbs were pricked with light.

'I'm scared,' he said.

'I'm going to stay with you all night,' I said. 'I just want to nick downstairs and get a Coke. Okay?'

When I got back he'd torn out the drip, the one they'd had so much trouble getting in because his veins had collapsed. It seemed

48

like there was a lot of blood.

'The fuck are you doing?'

'Help me, Lal,' he said. His eyes were dry. 'I don't want to stay here.'

'You'll get an infection.'

'I'll get one anyway.'

He listed in the bed, pressing a cotton patch to the crook of his arm where the shunt had been. I remembered, after the bone marrow transplant the first time, ten years ago, when he got pneumonia and almost drowned in his own lung-shit.

'Where do you wanna go?' I asked.

'Country,' he said. 'Out where the dish is. Do you remember that? When Nan took us?'

'Of course I do. But that's hours away. That's up near Forbes.'

'If you don't want to,' he said, 'I will take myself.'

'What about Theo?'

'I just want you to take me,' he said. 'I'm sorry. I'm sorry.'

'It's all right.'

I dressed him in clean clothes. I brought the car around, parked it in a five-minute zone while I went upstairs to sneak him out. I felt frightened, and it must have shown. It was the first time I'd seen him smile in days.

'We're not robbing a bank,' he said.

'You're supposed to *tell* them when you leave,' I hissed. If he could have laughed, he would have.

We drove all night. At first I talked to him to keep him awake. I was scared he'd drop off and slip away for good. But sleep dragged him down. I arranged my coat around him to cushion his body, leaned his car seat back. I could smell us both; my sweat and his chemicals.

'You gunna crash?' he croaked, when we'd been on the road

for some time.

'What? No,' I said, humourless, not understanding.

'Then can you take off my seatbelt? It's giving me the shits.'

The moon slipped away. I sang to myself to stay awake. I bought coffee and a chocolate bar at the servo. I had to help him sit on the toilet. He was too weak to stand up to piss.

Close to dawn I pulled into a truck stop.

'We're nearly there but I have to sleep, just for a bit,' I said. 'I'm knackered.'

I pushed my seat back, made myself a nest of jumpers and blankets.

'Tell me the story of the lead masks,' he said.

'I'll tell you when we get to the dish.' The sky was silver, the long grass very still. The roos were crouched by the highway.

He was shaking then and I knew I should have taken him to the closest base hospital, but I've always been glad I didn't.

TURNCOAT

The afternoons when Murray got home first, he liked to take the dog for a walk down the foreshore. In winter the fat palms shivered. Murray spent his days with trees. Naming them, measuring them, collecting the soil they stood up in. He'd lived in St Kilda for thirty-odd years, but sometimes the sour smells of rotting seaweed and dim sims and car fumes still surprised him. He had a habit of sniffing his fingers to see if they still smelled of forest at the end of the day. They never did, but sometimes his nails were still caked with soil.

The dog was a border collie named Quincy. Murray was engaged in a steady, patient strategy to win him over. He had a feeling the dog liked Lou better anyway but he kept trying. He had a feeling the dog was onto him.

Lou rang while they were out walking.

'You down the beach?' she said. 'It sounds windy.'

'Just on our way home. How was your day?'

'Oh, a bit long. Got this really turgid letter from the Honourable Minister for Education. It's the death rattle. I reckon we'll be gone this time next year.'

Quincy stopped and started sniffing at the pavement. Murray let him.

'You're sounding a bit nihilistic there, Louise.' He was hurting in his joints like he might be coming down with the flu.

'I'm calling it like it is. The union's gone to shit. Nobody cares about these kids.'

'Well, maybe not those wankers on Spring Street, but—oh, Quincy, mate—' he grimaced. 'Your dog is hanging a whacking great turd. On the pavement outside the Espy.'

'*My* dog.'

Murray was happy he'd got a laugh out of her. He thought he was getting better, after all these years, at listening for the signs and signals. He'd been in love with Lou for a long time, but he was still scared of the sorrow of which she was capable.

At work, out in the forests, the first thing they did was choose a centre point, hammer in a star picket, run a tape out in cardinal directions. They could only hope that what they measured in that circle-plot patch was representative of the surrounding bush. Murray liked patterns he could read; liked trying to gauge things.

In their backyard, under the curve of the verandah roof, was an old church pew. Murray sat on it to pull off his boots. Inside at the kitchen sink he scraped half a tin of dog food into the metal bowl. It smelled foul; offensively meaty. He tipped in the leftover fried rice, then remembered dogs weren't supposed to have onion. He plugged his fingers into the rice and tried to find any shreds of the offending vegetable. He went outside with the bowl in his hands. The sky was like something from a renaissance painting.

'They're called stratocumulus,' he said to Quincy. He made the dog sit before he set the bowl on the bricks. He was aching all over.

He thought a bath might help. That's what Lou would suggest. He went into the bathroom and turned on the taps.

He looked at his soft belly, the stencil of his ribcage. His dick hung down limply. Only yesterday he'd had a good wank in almost exactly this position, bracing himself with one hand on the veneer of the sink, thinking about Lou's legs.

Murray stood looking at himself in the mirror. There was fine hair on the backs of his knuckles; bike-riding muscle clung to his legs. He shivered. The light in that room was like a doctor's surgery. Those stupid energy-efficient bulbs Lou bought. They took forever to come on, and then made everything anaemic and dull. The wind came in through the gap in the sash window and made a noise like a toothy whistle. The tiles were cold underfoot. How could he relax in there? He reached over and shut off the tap. He tugged at the rubber plug and everything drained away noisily.

He stood under the shower instead. Through the bubble glass he could still make out the outline of his own reflection in the mirror, skin slowly turning pink with the steam. He turned to face the shower head, cupped the water in his hands; splashed it over his head like a baptism.

Lou was home by the time he'd dressed again. In the kitchen, talking quietly to the dog, scratching his belly. Quincy lay spreadeagled.

'Bloody turncoat,' Murray muttered. Lou turned up her face to him like a naughty kid; did her disarming smile, still crouched.

She went on stroking the dog. Sometimes Murray wanted to write poems or songs for her, but he didn't know how. She was like a cigarette itch.

They were becoming older in symmetrical ways, both of them rangier and bolshier. He had the elegant sort of skull that was kind to thinning hair. She tried to sit up straight these days, to undo years of a tall woman's self-conscious hunch. Somehow they had always managed to coordinate their spasms of melancholia so that one of them kept it together. Hers were shorter, more acute, more frequent. Often precipitated by a tiny failure: a forgettable embarrassment.

It was happening again, Murray was sure. Last week they'd gone to a friend's book launch. She'd clutched her glass of wine with that private, terrible look on her face. Every time someone tried to make conversation, she'd slipped away and left him to do the work. He hated explaining her awkwardness. She knew it. She was always apologetic, always guilty after the fact.

'We can just go, Louie,' Murray had said. 'Tim won't care. We've said hullo. We've bought his book.'

'Can't. He's our friend,' she'd said, as though that explained it. They'd fought between the tram stop and their flat.

Now she straightened up, kissed him on the cheek. He couldn't even remember what that other Louise was like.

In the forest, in that theoretical circle plot they'd measured out, they had to work out the diameter of each tree. The universal standard was diameter at breast height. Lou had laughed the first time he'd described it to her; the way you had to throw a measuring tape around the trunk and catch it with the other hand, pull it tight to get a reading. 'Wouldn't want Hinch to hear about that,' she'd said. 'You're literally tree-huggers.' Murray was a shy romantic. He could throw his arms around a tree and work out how much

54

carbon was in a forest, but holding Louie, pressing his face to her neck, did not permit him to estimate anything.

Murray's sister came for tea. Lou had taken to inviting her more regularly, after the divorce had come through and her children had moved out. Lou insisted it wasn't pity: 'I just can't imagine going from a four-person household to living by yourself,' she'd snapped once, when Murray had asked, but he hadn't really seen the difference between that and charity. Lou had always gotten along well with his sister. She always remembered the kids' birthdays, what they were studying, where the boy was playing his gigs.

Lou made soup, and when she was slicing the bread she turned to say something and the breadknife nicked her fingertip. There seemed to be a lot of blood. It dripped over the bread and the cutting board, and ran into the lines of her palm when she held up her hand in shock.

'Let me get a look,' Murray said. She'd cut a jagged flap of skin from the tip of her middle finger.

'Have you got elastoplasts in your bathroom?' asked his sister.

'Yes, but we've got *no bread*,' Lou said in a panic, and they all laughed.

Whenever his sister started on about menopause, Murray kept his mouth shut and listened for Lou's empathetic murmur. He was grimly fascinated by the way they spoke. When he was a child his mother, then his sister, too, had burned their sanitary napkins in the incinerator in the backyard. He remembered watching them from the doorway, poking the soiled stuff with a stick. He didn't really understand the way any of it worked, but something about that memory of his mother and sister standing there by the incinerator at dusk made him think of bleeding as a ritual, something secret and pyrrhic. He'd tried to explain it to Lou once. *Nothing too mystical about it*, she'd said. *It's a sort of dragging pain at the tops of your legs.*

Murray and Lou stood in the kitchen after his sister had left.

'The way she talks about it—it's almost like a grieving process, isn't it,' Lou said thoughtfully, drawing the tea towel in between her fingers. 'I've never even thought about it like that. Isn't it funny. None of us understands one another at all.'

She flung the cloth over one shoulder like a waitress; turned back to the sink. Murray watched the shadows on the back of her neck as she scrubbed.

'You're beautiful, Louie,' he said.

She looked up in surprise. She was already grinning. 'When I'm doing the dishes.'

Out in the forest, once they'd measured the trees, they moved on to the other parts of the ecosystem. There was a way of breaking down the bush into the trees, the shrubs, the herbs and grasses, the litter—the leaves and sticks—the fallen boughs. Last was the foot of soil underneath it all. They measured everything; left holding armfuls of brown paper bags filled with leaf litter, cores of soil.

Murray wanted to say, *Don't be sad, Louie*, but it didn't seem to fit. She looked indefatigable, pushing her hair back from her forehead with the back of her hand; she looked placid. Had he dreamt it? He felt unwell.

'I might jump in the shower before bed,' he stammered.

'Okay,' she said. She glanced at him over her shoulder again. 'You all right? You look a bit grey.'

'Yeah, yeah.'

He set the tap running. He stripped off his clothes quickly, and tried not to look at himself in the mirror, but that made it worse. He shut off the tap and sat on the edge of the bath. The cold enamel dug into his bum. He put his head in his hands.

'You all right?' Lou's voice floated in under the door. 'Murray? Don't bloody pass out in there.'

'I'm okay,' he said. 'Can't a man take a shower by himself?'

The water was pooled at his ankles. He sniffed his hands. They smelled like nothing at all.

Midweek he had to drive out to bushfire country. In the morning he and Lou fucked sleepily. She reached for him like a lucid dream; froggy hands, stale breath. He was barely awake when he came. Afterwards she sat on the toilet and complained about the tiles being cold under her feet, and gave him a torpid leadlight smile, exactly like that Ray Carver poem. He almost told her that. The first time he'd come as a kid, he'd thought there was something wrong. It had frightened him that he was capable of it. He'd called for his mother, panicked, hand still clutching his cock. His mother wasn't home. He'd thanked God regularly for years afterwards. Remembering it even now made him ache with embarrassment. He'd told Lou *that* before. She'd laughed like a child.

After all these years Murray was still struck by that immediate disorientation that came with a new site, walking in circles, lining out tapes. It all looked the same. There was no north, no south. All the trees were mountain ash at first. He liked mapping out the people, too. The ecological researchers were young and efficient; they did things by the books. They spoke less, worked cheerfully. The old boys were quiet to begin with, but they got to talking as the day wore on. Then the fieldwork moved slower. They'd stop to lean against the trunks, watch the researchers measuring leaf litter or diameters, and theorise on relationships. By the end of the day, Murray was always so familiar with the site that he'd wonder how he was ever disoriented. He liked working with the CSIRO blokes, who insisted on taking a six-pack of Melbourne Bitter—though they were all from Canberra—in the ute fridge. At the end of each day they had a sort of debrief before they went back to the motel. Murray liked the ceremony of that.

At night he mostly ate dinner by himself, then phoned Lou lying on top of the bed.

'How's the motel?' she asked.

'Pretty flash. WIN news programs, floral quilt. Little plastic bag of bickies and all.'

She laughed. It was an old joke of theirs, making his work travels more exotic than they were. 'You know what they do have, though,' he went on, 'is a really good globe in the bathroom.'

'Are you being funny?'

'Not in the slightest. It's sort of warm light. Makes you look *fantastic*. I think I might get one for our bathroom.'

'All right,' Lou said. The way she just let it go made him furious. Murray wanted her to understand: that energy-efficient globe was horrible, it was driving him mad. She started talking about the letter she'd been asked to draft on behalf of the staff, something about a funding profile, she might see if she could write a piece for *Crikey* or somewhere like that.

'The problem is, none of them have got much fight left, they're all so burnt-out.' She paused. 'Fiona said today "I wish the kids knew how hard we were pushing". But they can't—they're kids, that's it.'

'It's really enough that they go to school,' said Murray absently. He held one hand to his nose, but his fingers just smelled like cheap soap. 'How's Quince, anyway?'

Driving back into the city he stopped at a big lighting store. He stood in front of all the globes and chewed his thumbnail. He ignored all the energy-efficient bulbs. The LED ones were expensive. He thought the bathroom had a bayonet fitting, but he couldn't be sure. Maybe he should call Lou. He felt helpless.

A kid with a name badge and a haircut he recognised as trendy approached him, asked if he wanted a hand.

'Lot of choice, isn't there,' Murray mumbled.

'The LED ones are good. They only use about ten per cent the energy of your traditional bulbs.'

'Just give me a second, will you, mate. I'll let you know if I need anything.' It came out meaner that he'd meant it to, and Murray instantly wanted to apologise, but the kid's smile didn't waver.

'No worries. Take it easy,' he said. Murray went back to the little boxes. Even the incandescent bulbs had names and codes he couldn't understand. He flipped his car keys over in his hand.

Lou phoned when he'd just arrived home, but the line was breaking up and he couldn't understand her.

'—branch meeting last night—' she was saying.

'What?' Murray said desperately. 'Louie, I can't hear you. Will you be home soon?'

'—quarter to six,' she said, and disappeared with a crackle. Murray looked at the dog.

'It's too cold to go down the beach now, Quince,' he said. 'Why don't we just have some tea and call it a day.' It was almost dark. Lou had marked the shortest day of the year on their calendar in the kitchen, and he'd been watching it draw nearer.

He went to the shed for the stepladder. He fitted the new bulb. The light was better. He took the old, energy-efficient one outside and hurled it into the bin. It made a satisfying noise. Was that dangerous? He couldn't remember. The bath was ready. He dipped a foot into the water. His skin hurt; he was aching all over. He lowered himself into the tub and closed his eyes.

Keys in the door, Lou's boots in the hallway.

'You home?' she called.

'Yep.'

'Where are you?'

'Bathroom.'

'Dana can't use her MSO tickets tonight. *Eine kleine Nachtmusik.* Do you feel like going?'

He wrung out the facecloth. He didn't answer.

She appeared in the doorway. 'I've just had the most beautiful walk home,' she said. Her cheeks were red. 'All the stars were out. Just this *bitter* wind.'

'Doesn't sound too flash.'

'The way the clouds were moving,' she said, 'made it look like the moon was falling.' She was breathless. He knew it then: one day soon they'd be friends. He wanted to say it out loud. He wanted to tell her, like the morbid facts they read to each other from the newspapers. Inexorably rising sea levels; endangered animals.

'You hardly ever have baths,' she said. She took off her woollen hat and let her hair fall down. She turned to the mirrored cabinet above the sink and scrunched her fingers at her scalp. He could see her reflection in the mirror. She was ready for him to say something funny. She turned back to him expectantly.

He felt his mouth go slack. 'I think I'm crook, mate,' he said. 'I think I'm getting crook.'

He brought his hands to his eyes. Tepid water splashed up his forearms.

'Okay. It's all right,' he heard Lou say.

'I'm scared,' he said. He pressed his palms hard against his eyelids. Pinpricks of light swarmed across his vision. No Louise, only those terrible stars.

She was stroking his ears with flat palms, like she might comfort a dog. He could feel her breath on his cheek. She was very close.

'You're okay,' she said.

'I know. Stupid.'

'Not stupid, Murray, fuckssake.'

He opened his eyes. Lou looked relieved.

'Did the bulb go in here?' she asked. 'Light's changed.'

DOGS

Usually we took turns but sometimes Foggo wanted her to himself.
Once he called it, that was it.

Foggo had the car, so he was the boss. It belonged to his dad,
but his dad was dead. Foggo was also the biggest, though Willy
was catching up. Everyone thought of Foggo as the biggest,
anyhow.

China wasn't Chinese. His mum was Malaysian or Maltese or
something. His dad was Vietnamese, and everyone knew he made
drugs. Speed and E. There was a weird thing where China didn't
talk about it, and none of us had ever seen Mr T at work, but
everyone knew. It wasn't just the kids. All the parents said it, too.

Nicky was the smallest but he had the most to say. He had this
way of cracking you up just by looking at you. I reckon he was the
smartest of the lot of us, but he never let on.

Willy's family had a dishwasher and an Xbox. His parents taught at the Catho school. He was the sort of kid who used to be scrawny and cop shit for it, and then he got bigger and won best and fairest three years in a row.

On Fridays we'd pull up outside the pub and the girls'd be standing outside waiting for us. You could have your pick. Foggo would drive by and look at them all huddled there, like a police line-up, smoking and touching their hair. If he didn't see anything he liked he'd bite his thumbnail and say, *dogs, fucken dogs, mate*, and we'd all agree, and we'd roar out of there. On to Maccas or the river or someone's house, if we knew there was something going on.

The trophies were China's idea. I didn't really get it. It wasn't like we ever looked at them. Mostly they went in the console or the glove box, but a few things—like Casey Grimes' gold necklace with the cross, or one of those detachable bra straps we think came from Steph Horsburgh—a few things, we hung from the rear-view mirror. The gold cross creeped me out. It was only the size of a five-cent coin, but at night it glinted under streetlights.

I also thought it was weird that none of the girls ever asked for her shit back. Like, maybe Courtney Wyatt didn't care she'd left her undies on the back seat of Foggo's dead dad's car, or maybe she was too embarrassed. But I was always surprised about Casey's necklace. She went to school with Willy's sister. I saw her around a bit after that night we took her for a ride, but I never saw her with another cross. Probably her mum or dad gave it to her. Shit like that made me feel bad, but it wasn't the sort of thing you could say to the other guys.

• • •

I used to think we never did it with girls who didn't want it, but one time there was a chick said we'd forced her. 'Chicks are like that,' Fog said. 'They feel bad afterwards, so they try to make it better for themselves.' That's what my dad told Mr Wye when we all got called into his office after school that time. Willy's dad was mad as a cut snake, but the rest of the dads just laughed. China's old man didn't even show. It was stinking hot that day. I remember the wormy track of sweat down the side of Mr Wye's head. Afterwards we rode down the river. Something must've spooked us a bit, because none of us spoke till we were there. Then Fog laid down his bike and said, 'She wanted it,' and we all went, *Yeah*, and Fog said, 'Fat cunt. Just about had to roll her in flour to find the wet spot,' and we all said the way we remembered it till we were sure it was right.

Foggo had this way of testing us. When we skated he'd get us to do bigger and bigger tricks. He wasn't the best at it—Nicky was—but he had no fear. When we started getting over skating, since none of us could do that many tricks anyway, he began to light the ramps on fire. He'd pour petrol in a ring on the ground, or dribble it in a line along the concrete benches in the park where we used to try darksliding.

He made things more exciting just when we were getting bored. Like one time I was dumb enough to tell China I thought Despina Vasilakis was hot. He told Foggo. One night we're drinking on the oval and Fog pulls up with Desi in the car. We all sit around on the cricket pitch. For some reason we've got extra grog, and we've done some nangs, and we're all fucked. Desi's sitting across from me. I can hardly look at her, she's that beautiful. Her breath comes out in clouds. She's got half a smile on her face like she's waiting for the end of a joke. She whinges once or twice about the cold, and finally Willy gets a tarp from the car to put around her. Whenever she reaches for the bottle she makes a plasticky rustling sound. When Fog starts kissing her I'm pissed, but I know I'm gunna get my turn, so I'm waiting. Thing is, Desi's hard work. She's drunk and real floppy. Once she even spews everywhere— mostly on herself and on the tarp, but Foggo's lucky he gets out the way in time. When it's my turn her face is pressed to the grass, in her own spew. I've got two fingers in and she's not even looking at me. She's making this whiny noise. The guys are watching and I can't get hard. I have to get myself going. Fog and Nicky are pissing themselves. When I finally come it's a relief. Desi probably won't remember it but I won't forget it, because I really wanted to do it different with her.

She had frizzy dark hair that she made straight, but there were always these little fluffy baby hairs round her forehead. Killer legs and this huge smile. Now when I think of her, it's Bundy vomit and blue tarp. After school she moved to Melbourne to go to uni. She was really smart. Her undies were white with a satiny yellow rosebud, smaller than my fingernail, on the front. China nicked the flower. He hooked it into the clip of the bra strap. Seeing it made me feel crook, so after a while I put it in the glove box with some of our other stuff.

The last time it happened there was nothing for us to keep. Foggo, Nicky and I were cruising, waiting for Willy to finish work, waiting for China to answer the phone. We parked out the front of the bottle shop. Foggo went in. Nicky and I waited underneath the lit-up sign. Nicky kicked at the pebbles. His fidgeting drove me mental. I watched Foggo talking to the guy behind the counter.

He came out holding the plastic bags. A lot of Jimmy, a pack of cigarettes, plus whatever else he'd stuffed down his pants. He held out his hand for money. I looked over his shoulder at the guy behind the counter. He waved at me. I didn't wave back.

'I got an idea,' Foggo said. He sounded like he did after one of his crazy sprints up the guts, kicking one on the fly from outside fifty. He was fast for a big guy. 'You wait here. I'll be back. Tell Willy we'll meet him at the park.'

'What one?'

'Fuck, Nicky, the one near the airfield. The one we fucken always go to, you dumb cunt.'

'How the fuck's Willy gunna get there?' I asked.

Foggo shrugged. He opened the car door, stood with a hand on top. 'Just tell him to meet us. It'll be a surprise.'

'At least give us some durries to have now, cunt,' Nicky said. Foggo threw him the whole pack, then pitched two tinnies at me. He chucked them overarm out the car window so hard I almost dropped them. The car roared off and I thought, *He'll get pinged by the cops.*

We walked up the road to the payphone and called Willy. He was just finishing his shift at the IGA. Marissa Markovic answered the phone and Nicky chewed her ear off so long I had to put in another forty cents. I heard her laughing down the line. We walked back to the bottle-o car park and started to drink. Nicky was talking shit. He got up and started to pace a bit, toeing at the pebbles below the lit-up sign again. I said, 'Fuckssake, Nicky, can you keep still. You got a worm or something?' He just laughed.

'Can't help it,' he said. The white bits of his eyes were shining. He was hopping from one foot to the other now.

'What, you gotta take a piss, mate? Fog's gunna love that, fucken ballet dance.'

'Stop tryna be him, cunt,' Nicky said. But we grinned at each

67

other. I liked Nicky even when he was a pain in the arse.

We'd finished half the pack of cigarettes by the time Foggo got back. I heard his car ages before I saw it, hole in the muffler. He pulled in by the bottle shop. He stuck his head out the window.

'Fuck you been?' Nicky called.

'Had to go to the servo,' said Fog. He was doing a smile that made him look nuts. China was sitting next to him. I stomped my empty can of Jimmy and yanked open the door. Willy's sister was in the back. She was still in her striped school dress and rugby jumper. I saw she'd pulled the sleeves down over her fingers.

'Where's Will,' she said. She looked right at me. White-blue light on her, the kind of light that shows up your veins. I got a bad feeling in my guts. I tried to make my face say sorry.

'Settle down, Missy,' Foggo said. 'I told you already. He's gunna meet us.'

'I don't believe you,' she said. Her voice was like cut glass.

Fog looked at her in the rear-view mirror. He raised his shoulders. 'All right. Don't.' He turned to me. 'You gunna get in, or just stand there?'

I got really mad then. She wasn't even the sort Foggo liked—big tits, big bum. Girls that looked like women. Missy was tall but narrow, like there were parts of her that didn't realise they were supposed to grow. She kept her nails short for netball. And she was too young to hang out the front of the pub. Fog was only doing it to fuck with Willy.

'Fog,' I said. 'This is fucked.'

'I don't care if you're gunna be a pussy, but either get in or don't,' Foggo said.

'You going or not?' Nicky said to my shoulder blades. I walked around to the passenger side and opened the door. China got out with a shitty look on his face and slid in the back, and Nicky followed. Missy was pressed right up against the window like she couldn't get far enough away from either of them. China passed her a tin, but she wouldn't take it.

'He's just being friendly,' Fog said. He was still watching in the rear-view mirror. The gold cross was spinning and sending off points of light.

'Where are we meeting Will?' Missy asked.

'He's being friendly,' Fog said again. 'No need to be a bitch about it.'

He pumped the pedal so fast my neck snapped back, hit the part of the seat where the headrest should've been. He saw. He smirked. I wanted to kill him.

Willy was already there when we got to the park. I saw his mum's car, which he wasn't meant to borrow on Friday nights. Fog rolled down his window, revved the engine.

'We going to the airport?' Willy called. He didn't even look in the back seat. Fog gave him a thumbs-up and floored the accelerator again. Willy's lights flicked on and he followed us up the road. The airfield was closed for the night. They'd re-fenced it all about three years before. Used to be you could only get in if you climbed through a hole in the cyclone wire, but then one time we brought equipment and cut the padlocks on the side gate, and either they hadn't noticed or they didn't care, because they never fixed it. Missy went, *Jesus, fuck!* when we went over the ditch. I reckon her head coulda hit the ceiling. China got out and pushed open the gate. He took a piss standing by the fence.

We parked on the runway, the two cars side by side. Willy got out grinning. He was in the scuzzy trackies he wore to work, and he looked extra lanky.

'You boys been up to much?' he called. Then he looked in the back seat of Foggo's car and saw Missy. 'Fuck's this?'

'Thought we could do something different, eh?' said Foggo.

'I'll smash your fucken face in.'

'What's the matter? You don't want a turn, mate? You wanna sit this one out?'

The car door swung open and Missy fell out onto her knees like a stroke patient. I didn't even see her get up, she was that quick. She just took off sprinting. Her dress was hitched up around her undies. Her hair had come loose. It was flying behind her like a flag. She didn't need to run that fast. Fog would've followed through if she'd stayed there, but he wasn't the sort to chase a girl down, usually. Willy ran after her, then stopped, like he knew he'd never catch her. He yelled her name with his hands cupped round his mouth, then he turned to face Foggo.

'You fucken dog,' he said. His fists rained on Foggo's face before Foggo thumped him in the guts. Willy doubled over. I heard the air go out of him. But he stood up. He and Foggo circled each other. Fog's nose was bloodied, but he looked massive. I'd been thinking Willy was catching up to him. I'd forgotten Fog's mongrel rage. He could swell to twice his own size.

Willy swung wildly, like he'd never been in a fight in his life. He clipped Foggo's jaw. Foggo drew back once. He smashed Willy in the side of the face, and that was it. Willy went down. He put his hands over his ears and lay there. Fog was kicking him in the ribs, in the guts. Finally China and me got it together enough to pull him away. Fog said, *Get the fuck off me.* He stood over Willy. He picked him right up by the shoulders, headbutted him. Willy fell to the bitumen again. Then he and China got in his dead dad's car and drove off.

Willy was face down. He turned his head a bit. His spit was gluey. I counted six teeth sprayed on the ground.

'Can you turn off the lights?' he said at last. His mouth didn't move right. There was blood coming from his ear and his eyebrow was split. I went to his car, switched off the headlights. Nicky was sitting by the driver's side, elbows on his knees. I chucked him the key.

I lay down beside Willy. The asphalt was holding the heat of the day. We were close to the fence, near the only section crowned with barbed wire. There was a shredded plastic bag caught there, flapping. 'Where do you reckon she went,' he kept saying, but real soft.

I don't remember who drove home. Probably me. I don't remember what Willy's parents said about his fucked-up face, one eye swollen shut, or the next time I saw Foggo. We all came apart after that.

The story is Missy went and hid in one of the drains. She was there for two days. No one had any idea where she'd gone. I dunno what Willy told his parents. On the Sunday night there was a bad storm, first real rain in almost a year. The drains flooded and she nearly drowned. Some old bloke found her by chance when he was out looking for his dog and drove her to the base hospital. Later she said she'd wanted to run away because she'd had a fight with her mum. That's what I heard, anyway. Willy's family moved not long after that. Someone said Wodonga, someone else said over the river, far as Griffith. Must have been a fair distance, because I've never run into him playing footy for anyone in the Mid Murray League since.

Nicky got done for arson around that time and went to juvie. He disappeared for ages, and when he came back he was a chippie with a wife and three kids. I see him round sometimes. He's quieter these days, Nicky, and you never see him without his family. His missus got him going to church. Once in a while we'll have a beer together.

71

China moved to the city after Year Eleven. None of us knows what happened to him. I used to say *Good day* to Mr T whenever I saw him until he died last year, but I never asked about China. I had a weird feeling they stopped talking.

Foggo had some rough years. I think it fucked him up when his dad died. But he came good. Last I heard he was a senior constable working at the Swan Hill station.

These days I'm with Naomi. There are times she won't open up for me, and I know it makes her feel bad. I say, *It's okay, baby.*

CONVALESCENCE

We left the hôpital Saint-Antoine at dawn. We stood on the pavement, cold and dumb. I heard the whale song of an ambulance fade sourly into the streets. It was Lewis who turned his back on the building first.

'Come on,' he said, with a jerk of his hand. 'Let's go home.'

I didn't want to go back to the apartment, but it was early and there was nowhere else to go. I asked if he wanted to get a coffee. He looked at me with an odd, tight expression.

'Why don't we go home, have a shower. I'll make us coffee if you want.'

We started moving as two machines. At the *métro* steps we laced fingers. The train was full of commuters, all dressed for work. We were coming home at the wrong time of day. I thought of all the mornings I'd walked home after a big night, still drunk, waving to cheerful neighbours out with their dogs. I thought of jetlag.

We looked at each other in the reflection of the train window. Lewis spoke to my image, sotto voce, *How's the pain*, and I said *Nothing*.

We didn't speak again until we got to Belleville, halfway up the hill.

'Almost there,' Lewis said, as though he were taking me somewhere I'd never been before. At the door he plunged his hands into his coat. 'The fuck did I do with the keys?'

'It's all right, I've probably got them.' I groped through my bag, whose contents shifted and slid over one another like things lost on the ocean floor. I dropped to my haunches. Lewis knelt beside me, palms upturned to receive the pens, scraps of paper, coins, lipstick, empty paracetamol tabs I handed him. My fingers were clumsy with cold. 'They're not here. You must have them.'

'I *don't*.' There was a frantic scratching in pockets. Further up the hallway, Mrs Bernardeau was locking her own door. Her older son Étienne stumped towards us, hitching his backpack.

'*'jour*,' he said as he passed. We smiled and murmured at him in unison. His mother paused at our door, clutching the squirming baby against her chest.

'*Ça va?*' she asked.

I nodded. '*Ça va, j'arrive pas à mettre la main sur mes clés—*'

Étienne was kicking the iron banister rhythmically. Mrs Bernardeau swiped at his arm and said, '*Ben, j'ai le double, si tu veux.*'

'What?' Lewis asked me. 'Does she have the super's number?'

My fingers closed around the keyring. 'Got them.'

Mrs Bernardeau smiled. She said goodbye to Lewis in English, and then she was gone, and we were still on our knees at the threshold of the door.

Inside, I set the kettle boiling.

'Why don't you get in the shower,' Lewis said. 'You'll feel better once you've warmed up.'

'You go.'

He did not take off his coat. We faced each other across the kitchen tiles.

'Are you all right?' I asked.

'Are you?'

'Yeah. You go first.'

He turned on the taps slowly, as would a guest. I heard the air groaning in the pipes, felt the pressure shuddering through the walls. I watched the news while I waited for him. A bad accident on the *périphérique*; a volcanic eruption in Iceland; a senior politician would admit to sending text messages to his secretary, but not to fucking her. The forecast for the day was fine, four degrees, with the threat of snow tomorrow. I switched off the television. My work was spread over the floor on my side of the bed, a mess of maps and illustrations and dense text. Yesterday morning Lewis had crouched there, barefoot, in the babel of paper, examining some delicate ink plan or other, flipping up and down the coloured sticky notes I'd daubed all over the photocopies. He was like a child fingering a lift-the-flap book that yielded no catchcry, no colour. When at last he'd got up and moved on, his feet had left small impressions in the paper, dimples all over Balzac and an illustration of the *Saints-Innocents*. It seemed a long time ago.

I gathered the papers and sat in the window to read until Lewis came out of the bathroom in a pearly haze of steam. I watched him dress. First the jeans that he retrieved from the floor and climbed into, stiffened to the shape of his long crooked legs, then a clean blue shirt. He rolled up his sleeves like a man ready for a task of work.

At the hospital they'd offered us pamphlets. The doctor had said, *I can recommend an English-speaking grief counsellor,* and I'd said, *It's okay. It wasn't something we'd planned.* The doctor started to say that it didn't matter, that everyone responds differently. This was when Lewis had gone to get a coffee. I said, *We were—I was going to have a termination.* The doctor had nodded. He'd said, *There's still room for grief.* I'd asked him when I could return to work.

Lewis flicked on the television again. He sat on the bed to put on his socks, and looked at me with his hangdog eyes.

'I need to call the university,' I said. 'Tell them to cancel my class this afternoon.'

'Want me to do it?'

How? I almost snapped, but didn't. He was trying to find a use for himself. He lay back and rubbed his face.

'Fuck, what a weird night,' he bellowed. My eyes were leaking. He looked up at me. 'Oh. Hey. I'm sorry.'

'Don't be,' I said. 'I don't know why I'm crying. Must be some weird hormonal thing. I feel fine.'

'Come here,' he said.

I stood with my clothes bundled in my arms. 'It's okay,' I said. 'I'm okay.'

When I got out of the shower he'd found a Louis Malle film on the television. It was Jeanne Moreau, hopeless and handsome in a rain-drenched street. We'd seen it before, a few years back, at a festival. He'd liked it for its Miles Davis soundtrack. I'd liked it for its femme fatale.

'It's that movie,' he said, 'you know.'

I lay with my head in the crook of his arm, not quite comfortable. I dozed for a while. When I woke he was still holding me. I thought about my mother. I thought about Lewis. He'd played a show in a red cave of a bar the night before last. Lewis's is not the kind of music the French will listen to. *Trop compliqué*, says my friend Guillaume, pushing his lips into a flower. Our friends had been kind enough to come anyway; to watch politely while Lewis coaxed stories from his guitar. Going home on the train afterwards, Lewis had sat with his guitar case between his legs and we'd laughed in that weepy, private way.

The trumpet was still keening from the television. I sat up.

'Let's get out. Let's go and do something. We won't be here much longer.'

'Where do you want to go?'

I suggested we go to the catacombs. He'd never been.

'A cemetery,' he kept saying. 'Today, of all days.'

'It was just an idea. Don't worry about it.'

'Look, if you want to go, I'll come with you. It's just—'

'Why is today such a bad day to go? I don't want to just sit here.'

He looked at me like his patience was fading. I was feeling mean. I wanted to pick a fight.

He didn't take the bait. He said my name instead. I lay down again, faced the wall.

'How're you feeling?'

'Fine,' I said, 'I feel bulletproof.'

'You hadn't actually made the appointment. For the termination.'

'Well, no, but we'd decided, hadn't we.'

Lewis's body was warm. His face was at my neck.

'It would be very normal to feel sad,' he said into my hair.

'You can't feel sad about something you didn't want.'

'Okay. Okay, Tess.' He rolled away to the other side of the bed.

We were discovering in each other new shapes and colours, strange prisms of blue that we never knew existed.

•   •   •

We did go to the catacombs in the end. At the entrance he stopped short and read, in a dramatic version of his schoolboy accent, *ARRÊTE! C'EST ICI L'EMPIRE DE LA MORT* where it was carved above the doorway. He did a little laugh.

It was clammy down there in the earth. Lewis held my hand until we had to walk single-file, shouldering skulls.

'Ever touched one?' he asked. He put out his hand and cupped a smooth forehead. 'Wonder who this was.'

We stopped from time to time to read the inscriptions and the quotes, or to admire the bones stacked so lovingly, so symmetrically, in the jaundiced light.

'It gets a bit much, doesn't it,' he said as we neared the end. 'You start to get a bit desensitised to it, you start to want some fresh air.'

We burst into the chalky daylight a mile away from where we'd started. We looked at each other, stunned.

Underground again, but in the *métro*, we walked past the string section that sometimes plays at Châtelet. There was a thickness of people. I lost sight of Lewis. The strings were playing Wagner, the prelude from *Tristan and Isolde*, which I only recognised because Lewis loved it. I might have stood there watching for a minute or two before I remembered we were separated in the crowd. I saw his untidy dark head. He dropped some change into the open cello case and hurried out of the way, to the back of the crowd. He turned his face to the wall. I watched him from across the passageway. Right there I felt as if I'd relinquished something.

The doctor had left the two of us alone so I could make the translations.

'They've offered me a D and C,' I said.

'A what?'

I explained it to him.

'I always just thought it happened by itself,' Lewis said.

'Sometimes it does.'

He looked twelve years old. I thought about how strange it was, all these secret things that women know, and how men might never learn them.

'It's just that it's over with quicker this way,' I said.

'And they'll give you a general.'

'It'll only take ten minutes. Then they'll probably keep me a few hours. You may as well go home for a bit. Get some sleep. I can call you when it's over.'

'Don't be ridiculous,' he'd said. 'Jesus, Tess.'

I should have said something nice then, but I only turned on my side to look out the window. It was night. The fluoros on the hospital ceiling were reflected in the glass. They made neat rectangles. There'd been nothing else to see where I lay.

In the train we took seats side by side. Lewis touched the back of his hand to mine. Our knuckles kissed lightly.

'Are you hungry?' he asked. I shook my head.

'I think we should get something,' he said. 'We haven't eaten since this time yesterday.'

'Okay.'

I was tired but I didn't want to go back to the apartment. We got off at République. I think he meant to head towards Guy's resto, but realised that we'd have to do the explaining—why I wasn't teaching this afternoon, why we'd missed dinner at Aurélie's the night before—and thought better of it. We ended up at a bistro near the canal. Lewis wolfed down his soup, but we sat for a long time afterwards. He started one of his lovely, absurd letters. I watched him, hand skidding over the foolscap as he tried to organise and describe everything he'd seen, resurrecting it all from the compost of memory. Occasionally he'd look up. 'Where was that funny place we saw the band last week?'; 'What was the name of that thing Alice cooked for us?' Crinkly eyes: he was being witty. I'd had four cups of coffee and I could feel my heart throbbing. At last he leaned back from the table.

'Do you want to wait here a minute?' he asked. 'I won't be long.'

I sat by the window while he ran across the street. I ordered a glass of wine and opened the paper. There was a story about a Russian man who had planned to commit suicide by jumping off a bridge. When he got there he'd met a woman with the same intention. Now, the article reported, the two were to marry. I read it twice. I thought I might show Lewis. Perhaps he'd get a song out of it. Perhaps he'd get one out of today. Perhaps I'd recognise us, months later, in a nest of words he'd leave on the kitchen table for me to read. Not long now before we'd be back home, standing at the back of the same gigs, power-pedalling up the same hills, kissing on the same street corners. There'd be talk of moving up the country. There'd be months of him working, alone with his songs that sprawled like stories, like galaxies; a humming in his skull. Then all the shows, all the glory of dusky pubs. Strange, the way we revealed ourselves to each other in small, shy flashes, even after all this time. He'd come to Paris with me because he was my fella. I'd got the research grant, it was what I'd wanted. *Anyway*, he'd said at the time, *haven't you followed me round for years?* He'd made an adventure out of it, remained good-natured even when he was pulling pints in an Irish pub and playing open-mic nights for free; he who'd played sold-out shows back home. I couldn't imagine going back. There was so much that I wanted, but it was here, in this city, where Lewis could only tread water.

He returned looking pleased with himself, head bowed into the collar of his coat, package tucked under his arm. He sat back down opposite me and handed me the paper bag. Wrapped inside layers of tissue was the treasure he'd bought in secret: a cardigan, thick-knitted lambswool the colour of smoke. I put it on straight away. He was happy that he'd made a good choice.

'You can take it back,' he said shyly. 'If you don't like it, or—you want something else.'

'No, it's beautiful. I love it.' I leaned across the table to kiss his mouth.

The waiter swept by, made genial comments about lovers and luck as he cleared our cups.

'*Vous avez de la chance,*' he said, 'you look after each other. You keep her warm and she does the talking, *hein*?'

He winked at Lewis, clapped him on the shoulder. He stood and talked for a while. Where were we living? For how long? What did we do?—all the while the cups tittering quietly in his hands. He liked us. They all did.

'It's going to be a fine afternoon,' he said when he brought us the bill. 'The clouds are going to disappear.'

We both looked up as we left the café. Anaemic sky.

'Do you feel like going up to Sacré Cœur?' I asked. 'If it's going to be a fine afternoon.'

'Are you up for it?' he asked. 'You're not flagging?'

'Yes.'

So we caught the *métro* in the wrong direction; not back home, but to that great white elephant on the hill. I loved the view from Sacré Cœur almost more than anything else in the entire city. Lewis loved the basilica itself. He was not religious, but he'd told me about the first time he visited the cathedral. 'I broke down,' he'd said. 'I just understood completely how people *did* believe in God back then. Imagine if you were alive when that was being built. How could you not believe in God?'

When we surfaced in Pigalle, the sun was low in the sky and the streets were awash with a sleepy orange light. Our shadows were oblique. Lewis's earlobes glowed red.

'I always reckon it's funny,' he said as we passed the Sexodrome, 'that they did the good Catho thing and put the Sacré Cœur as high up as they could, but then you've got all this shit sitting right under it. Bloody jelly dongs. And *Osez La Masturbation*.'

'It was the outer suburbs. The sex was here before the church was.'

'Yeah, I know, it's just—well, I guess it's pretty good, actually.' He laughed, bent his head to kiss me without slowing his pace. We could have been American tourists, strolling through the tired, gritty streets. We could have been anyone.

We let go our hands and did not speak as we started up the steps. Halfway to the top, I paused to look behind, to see the city taking shape at our heels. It was impatient, like a child sneaking a look at a Christmas present. Lewis turned around too, when he felt me drop away.

'Do you want to stop?' he called, a few steps ahead. 'You look like you're fading a bit.'

'No, let's just keep going.'

His strong, spidery legs took the stairs two at a time. I was slower. First there were four steps between us, then ten, and suddenly he was rushing ahead the only way he knew how, pulling away like an untamed horse, upward into the wide sky. He was a hands-in-pockets kind of walker, and there was something almost comical about his skinny figure, all in black, loping away from me. But the higher he got, the more enfeebled was I. He grinned and mouthed something at me, exhilarated, from the top. I pushed on, but crippled; I had the impression that I could topple back. Lewis was looking down on me. He'd stopped smiling. *It's all right,*

I wanted to say before he could ask it. I made a silly joke. He laughed unsteadily. I set one foot in front of the other.

And when I reached the top at last, he held me very tightly. The view I had was of his coat, a sliver of the apricot-coloured afternoon past his shoulder. We might have stood like that for ages, clenched and petrified, but after a time we unfolded. He put an arm around me and we stood in the shadow of the basilica. The clouds had lifted and the city spread its legs for us; all the factories, all the rooftops, the square where the abattoir once was, the cathedrals and hospitals and spires and stations, all steeped in gold.

'It's going to be all right,' he said without looking at me. 'We're almost there.'

We stood there, shoulder to shoulder. We were Marie and Pierre in Zola's *Paris*, looking out over the city at the novel's end. *Du blé, du blé partout, un infini de blé...*

All this beauty, all this gold. I turned to him, I wanted to tell him. *There's this priest*, I wanted to explain, *who has a complete loss of faith,* une crise de foi totale, *and so he leaves the monastery and meets this girl, Marie, and...*

It was too hard.

'What?' he asked. He dropped his head. 'What did you say?'

So much beauty, so much gold. It was pornographic.

'I said,' I answered, 'I said, "this is too hard."'

VASELINE

Delaney's mom has bought tampons for me since I was twelve because I've always been too embarrassed to ask Pop or Luther. Delaney brings them to school for me in the drugstore paper bag. Last time she gave me a jar of Vaseline, too, and told me it'd make it hurt less next time Ray tried to stick it in me. The Vaseline had a blue strip on its lid to show that it hadn't been opened. It snapped apart easy enough. The surface of the jelly inside was smooth, calling out for me to plug my finger in it. It smelled like glue or something else you might use around the house. I put it in my bedside drawer. Luther wasn't around to find it and ask me about it. He was in Colorado.

In the summer, before he left, we hung out almost every day.

We drove to Angel Peak, parked in the campground. Up there

it was always noisier than I expected. The wind was loud. Depending which way it blew, you could hear the compressors down below, thumping away like an irregular heartbeat. We stood there while it got dark and I said, *I hope I never get used to this* and he looked at me all embarrassed.

We went to visit Mom, which we hadn't done together for a long time. The cemetery is tiny. It almost got eaten up by the gas plant, but somehow survived. It's closed in with a chainlink fence, edged by road on two sides and by the plant on the other two. There's a sign that reads ST MARYS CEMETERY in skinny iron letters, no apostrophe. Maybe someone didn't think it was worth it, or maybe the small things are hard to make. The main Bloomfield cemetery has one identical.

It was a concession for Pop to have her buried at St Mary's, and not in the big cemetery on the hill. He was raised Episcopal. In the end he said, 'It's not about me or what I want,' and that was all. He works at the ConocoPhillips plant next door. He visits Mom every afternoon when he leaves. They're mostly Latino names on the graves, with shrines to saints on top. Mom's is smaller. She liked things plain. Anyway, Luther had suggested it and we went together. It was the middle of the week, late afternoon. We were the only ones there. I laid the plastic flowers I'd brought. I left Luther to say what he wanted. I walked between the graves. The white and silver of the tanks was almost blinding. I didn't think I was scared of heights, but when I saw the stairs winding up those tall towers, I got a bad feeling at the tops of my legs. I bent to wipe dust off of my anklet and to check, from a distance, if Luther was still going.

We were walking back to the car when I saw a grave that read
TROY J "PEANUT" DEJESUS,
AUGUST 4 1979–NOVEMBER 27 1980.

I started to bawl. It came on so sudden. I couldn't say to Luther that I was crying about some stranger's dead baby. Mom had been gone for years. I think he was embarrassed. He walked ahead of me some, to give me a few moments extra to calm myself down before I got into the truck beside him. It was that New Mexico sky, electric blue. It looks the same every summer.

We drove to Morgan Lake, where we used to go fishing for carp and catfish, where the scenery was the coal power station. Of course you couldn't eat what you caught there, but that never was the point. I didn't like fish anyway. Mom used to fry catfish and serve it with cornbread and slaw. The small ones had dark flesh. They tasted muddy. Mom said that was because they came from the lake bed.

Luther and I stopped fishing there years ago, but we still drove out sometimes. The smog from the Four Corners plant hung so thick it was hard to see the mountains beyond. At dusk the sky was a sick pinkish colour. The lake was man-made. Its water was used to cool the power plant. It was on a Navajo reservation. Once I said to Luther, *It's sort of a shame for the Indians.* I meant the smoke spewing from the station. I meant the lake you couldn't swim in.

'They could've stopped it if they wanted to.'

'Actually they couldn't,' I said, but he wasn't interested. He was talking about how to break it off with his girl, since it was that time of summer when all the couples do that, since they'd all had a good hot two months of fucking and now they were going off to college so they had to practise saying *my high-school boyfriend* or *my high-school girlfriend*. If Ray goes off next year, maybe even if he doesn't, I'll be his high-school girlfriend. Names change, anyway. I'm Jessamyn when I'm at school, and Minnie when it comes out of Pop or Luther's mouth. Luther means 'soldier of the people'. It was Mom who liked it.

• • •

If someone had asked me I wouldn't have said we were especially close. But he was my brother. He taught me to drive. We ate dinner together every night of our lives. One winter, when we were little, we'd had chicken pox. We spent hours in an oatmeal bath, bored and irritable. We even watched porn together once. When I told Delaney that she shrieked, but it hadn't seemed weird at the time.

When Luther started talking about college, first Pop said, *What the fuck is in Denver*, then he said, *Okay*. By the time Luther got the scholarship he'd already come around to the idea. He started telling people, *Be a good thing for him to get out of this shithole town anyhow*, talking like Luther. I tried to close my ears when he got to talking like that. Mr Murphy my English teacher was always telling me to keep my grades up, but there's no football scholarship if you're a girl. Actually there's no Colorado, either, just endless hamburger dinners.

Pop and I stayed the night at a motel after we left Luther and all his things. It was on the outskirts of Boulder. I could tell Pop was tired. He lay on the bed watching *Jeopardy*. Earlier he'd talked about finding a Denny's for dinner but now it was looking unlikely. In the bathroom there was a strip of paper across the toilet seat like the seal on my jar of Vaseline, and a plastic tray of little soaps and bottles of shampoos. I washed my face at the basin. Pop stood behind me. He blocked out the light from the halogen in the hall. He said, *Don't you ever leave me like that, Minnie. I mean it*, and goddamn I knew he did. I said I wouldn't.

In the fall some crazy started going round attacking girls. One in the parking lot of the Economy Inn on East Main Street in Farmington, one a couple of streets back from the Greyhound station. A cheerleader walking home from Piedra Vista High.

I don't think any of us paid any attention. It was almost Homecoming, and we weren't talking about much else. Delaney's mom had said she'd drive us to Albuquerque to go shopping one weekend, only I was beginning to think she'd forgotten, and since she wasn't my mom I didn't like to ask.

Delaney lives in a trailer in Halliburton. When we were nine there was a spill that caused an acidic cloud. It wasn't as bad as everyone first thought, but she had to evacuate with her mom and her sisters. They stayed with her mom's boyfriend. He didn't like kids. Delaney said it was three days and he didn't look at her.

I don't remember that fluid spill at all. A few weeks after that my mom died. It was a stroke, an evil usually reserved for old people. Mom wasn't old. She was thirty-six. She hadn't smoked since college. Hers was from a blockage caused by loose brain tissue. Anyway, that was my fuel spill, that summer. When Pop tells the story he says, *She was dead before she hit the floor*. This is supposed to be comforting. What he means is, she felt no pain. What he leaves out is the blinding shock of it. It happened faster than a second. In this way, she forgot us.

After that guy grabbed the fourth girl our school made us all do self-defence classes. Just the girls, and just the sophomores up. I guess they either ran out of money for the freshmen, or else they didn't think he liked them real young. We stood in the gym in our sweatpants and snickered at the instructor. He told us about eye-gouging; swift heel of the palm to the nose; fingers to the throat, that hollow under the Adam's apple. He looked right at Delaney and said, *Do you walk home listening to your Walkman?* and she pushed her gum to the side of her mouth with her tongue and said, *Sir, I got no money for any of that shit*, but she said *shit* real quietly so he was embarrassed more than angry. He put us in pairs.

He made us attack each other. He even brought a couple pairs of swimming goggles so we could practise eye-gouging. He showed us different positions someone might attack us from. I kept forgetting the sequence of movements I needed to escape.

'I'd never remember any of this,' I said to Delaney.

'See how he hasn't mentioned the nuts yet,' she said. 'You think that's 'cause he's embarrassed to say *balls* to girls?' We were slapping at each other and laughing. The whole gym looked green through the goggles.

'Double dare you to raise your hand and ask him about it,' I said, and we clutched at each other.

The instructor told us to go limp if someone attacked us.

'Going dead-weight, that'll get him off guard,' he said. 'It's the limp noodle. It's all you have to remember. Drop to the ground.'

Delaney put her arms loose around my neck and leaned in close.

'Let's see if it works,' she whispered in my ear. Her breath made me shiver. I dropped to the gym mat. Her arms tightened around my neck. 'This is dumb,' she said. 'I could drag you off anywhere. It'd skin your knees is all.'

After school I waited for Ray by his truck. I looked at my face in his side mirror and tried to frown less. I lifted my chin. I leaned against the passenger door. He arrived with his buddies. They joked about me sitting in the front seat, but I jammed my backpack at my feet.

I said, 'Don't give me that shit. You all love sitting close back there. I heard about the locker rooms.'

Ray looked at me like he could have killed me, and the others were howling in the backseat, and Ray said, *You rather walk home?* and I said, *You bet I would.* Mostly because I knew he wouldn't pull over and make me get out with the guys in the back, but I was also that mad I would have walked the six miles if he'd let me out of the car. I had rage in my veins. If I were a boy I might've run around shooting things up.

He dropped off his buddies, but instead of turning off for my house, he doubled back to West Broadway and kept driving. When I asked where we were going he said, *I thought we could go up to Angel Peak*, which maybe sounds romantic the way I'm saying it, but actually meant he wanted to fuck. His hand was on my thigh.

We parked at the end of the lot. It was just us and a few RVs, but I couldn't see anyone around. Almost right away he got on top of me. He pulled my panties to one side in the way that meant he was in a hurry. I was bleeding so I thought maybe he wouldn't want to, but he did. It was the fourth day and all that was left was brown and I hardly think he noticed, anyhow. I wished he'd left the air on.

Afterwards we sat with our doors open. He rolled a blunt. I didn't feel like smoking but my hands smelled like his dick so I did it anyway. We talked about the creep who'd been attacking girls. I told him how they'd made us do self-defence at school. He looked at me surprised, like he couldn't imagine anyone ever doing that to girls like me.

'You know what I'd do if he tried a thing,' Ray said. When I didn't answer, he pointed his thumb and forefinger like a pistol.

'Ray, when you say shit like that it is so boring.'

'Shit like what? What is that supposed to mean?'

'What I said. I am so bored.' I yelled at the mountains. 'I—am—so—bored!'

'The fuck is wrong with you,' he said. He sounded disgusted. I got out of the truck. I climbed to stand on one of the picnic tables. I had a feeling Ray might drive off and leave me there, and I'd have to walk the fifteen miles home, but it was only fleeting. Ray could be a deadbeat, but he wasn't really mean. Actually he followed me. He sat down on the bench and held up the blunt. It was soggy between my fingers so I just held it a while and passed it back to him.

'I used to come here with Luther,' I said. 'Actually we used to go hunting for dinosaur bones but we never found any. Not even small ones.'

'You are so weird.'

I was standing with my arms stretched out. Ray smiled up at me, sun-sleepy. I knew then, really, that he would never drive away from me.

'Fuck it, baby,' he said. He held out his arms and I climbed into them, sat on his lap a second to kiss him.

I missed Luther more than I'd imagined. He called occasionally, but it wasn't the same. Things felt awkward when I couldn't see his face. Pop and I didn't have much to say to each other at dinner.

Luther had to keep up his grades to stay at CU. He was no scholar. He was no idiot, either, but I knew he worked slowly and gave up early. Seemed to me that stuff had trouble going in his ears. Once it got there, he never forgot shit.

For a while he had a girl who gave him pills to help him stay awake, get more done. They were really for kids with ADHD. He said everyone took them. I thought it was dumb, with his football, but when I said that he cut me down. The next time we spoke he wasn't going with that girl anymore and he didn't mention any magic pills. I didn't ask.

Meanwhile, it was almost Homecoming and I guess I'd talked about it enough that Pop realised he should give me some money to buy a dress, which he did, but it was fifteen dollars. I felt too bad to say anything. It wasn't his fault. How would he know how much a nice dress cost. I put the money in my underwear drawer and figured I'd borrow something from Delaney's mom.

In English we had to present our book reports. We'd been allowed to choose our books, but Mr Murphy had suggested one to me. Actually it was short stories, which I didn't know until I started it. It was mostly about unhappy couples who drank too much and argued. The fathers were all mean. I hadn't liked it, and I couldn't think of much I wanted to say except, *I wish they'd all quit bitching at one another*, but probably Mr Murphy had told me to read it because he liked it, so I pretended I enjoyed it. After class he stopped me and said my book report was very good, and would I like to try writing an essay for extra credit.

'No offence, sir,' I said, and then felt embarrassed about it. 'I mean, I don't want to sound rude, but I don't see the point.'

Mr Murphy said, 'Jessamyn, you've got to get out of here.' Then he put his hand on my ass.

When he saw my face he said, 'I'm sorry, that was my fault, I misread things. Please don't—please don't think I'm some dirty old creep.'

I looked at him carefully. I said, 'Mr Murphy. Don't worry.'

The way he was looking at me, I couldn't decide if he understood, or if he was about to kiss me. Then Mrs Vasquez knocked on the door.

'You ought to see Jessamyn's report on Carver,' Mr Murphy said. I felt like I'd imagined him touching my ass.

'Carver, that's advanced,' Mrs Vasquez said.

I looked at the picture of President Clinton behind her head.

'I'm trying to convince her to take AP English,' Mr Murphy said.

I was halfway to my locker before I realised I had my book report in my hand, which he was supposed to be grading. I stuffed it in my backpack. I already knew he'd never ask about it.

On my way home I stopped at the grocer. I stole a pack of Big Red, some hair elastics and an orange. Then I kept on down the street. I peeled my orange by cutting into it with my fingernails. The skin came away easy. I thought about my brother, jamming an orange quarter into his mouth, tropical wedge between his teeth like a cartoon smile.

I threw the peel into the gutter and went into the gas station and asked for a job.

Mom's things were still in our basement, mostly in zippered bags or those sturdy boxes. Some of them I remembered, but like from a dream—her blue swimsuit, or the ratty T-shirt with tropical fish on it, worn so thin you used to be able to see her nipples through it. Some of the things seemed like they belonged to a different mother, though. I didn't often have occasion to go looking through it all. Pop wouldn't have liked it.

Under a trash bag of her books from community college was a box of fancy shoes, then another filled with clothes. She was shy, and so were her dresses. My favourite was one that looked kind of olden-days, white cotton with long sleeves and lace teardrops hanging from the hem. It was soft with age. The waist was real low and loose. It came to my knees. It wasn't fashionable, but I hardly think it could have been fashionable when Mom wore it in the seventies. I stood in front of the mirror and made witch hands at myself. Wearing that dress made me dance in a jerky way. If Ray were here, he's say something like, *You're real fucking weird, you know that?* in that disgusted way of his, as if I'd shit on the floor of his truck. Actually I knew he'd hate the dress so I wanted to wear it.

• • •

Pop cried when he saw me in the dress the night of Homecoming. I felt bad, but I wasn't doing it to spite him. He took some pictures of me standing at the foot of the stair, and took some more when Ray arrived. Ray bought me a real nice corsage, tiny white and pink flowers. I think even Pop was impressed. He told Ray to bring me home by midnight, but it almost sounded like a joke. Some reason, those two get along well. I always think it's funny Pop trusts Ray but gets suspicious round Delaney's mom.

I phoned Luther before we left. He wasn't there, but that was okay. We hadn't arranged it.

I'd got Ray to buy liquor for me, which meant he'd got his brother to buy it. It was a plastic bottle of bourbon. When we got to school I slid it under the passenger seat in case his buddies came looking for some later. My hand touched something metallic. All I could think was, *What kind of dumbass bring a pistol to a Homecoming dance.* I didn't say it, though, since I didn't want to start something.

Delaney's guy was stoned. She was in a mood. Ray went straight to his buddies and they all stood there cracking jokes from the sides of their mouths. I knew he'd probably said something about my dress, since all the other girls were wearing strapless things, and he'd already told me I was weird in the car. The gym was decorated in blue and silver. It was all making me feel bitchy. I drank some punch. I listened to Delaney talk about Carter. I stood in the bathrooms and reapplied my lipstick. Karen Bridger was sobbing about something Donna Weitzman had said. I caught up with Ray right when a slow song came on. He acted like he was a real gentleman by asking me to dance.

I didn't want to move that way, that bored shuffle, the restrained bumping of hips. I could hold Ray's hands anytime. I wanted to dance the way Delaney and I did in her room. Legs set wide, the music throbbing all the way through to our heels, which would twitch and stamp, our wrists flicking like the belly-dancers we'd seen in movies. Sometimes we'd press our stomachs together like one of us was a guy, and I'd feel our hipbones knock. We made our hands soft and hard, flexed our wrists. Delaney's mom had been a dancer. She used to watch us and smoke and say, *Airy armpits, girls. You gotta have air under your armpits. That's what makes it look graceful.* Once she showed us what she meant. I never forgot it. She was drunk and the colour was high in her cheeks. Her body looked like a dancer's. She tossed her head. Her ribcage swelled and jerked. The way her hips moved made it look like she was fucking the air. Delaney and me weren't even embarrassed, since she didn't look like anyone's mom anymore.

I wanted to dance like that.

I was feeling good, like I could still drive. I had this idea I wanted to go up to Angel Peak. You can't see jack-shit at night, only points of light down where the town is spread, but I wanted to get out of that gym. By the time I came back, things would be winding down and we could either head to the canyon to drink, or else go to Camila Reed's party.

It wasn't hard to escape. Ray was holding my hand so lightly that I hardly think he noticed when I slipped away. My purse was under the bleachers with his keys stuffed inside. I had to pee real bad, but there was a line of girls waiting for the restroom. In the parking lot I squatted between two cars and hitched my dress up to my hips. I thought about when boys pee and you see steam. I was so cold. My jaw and shoulders and ass were clenched with it.

I was trying to remember where Ray had parked his truck. I looked at my face in the window of someone else's car. My hair was mussed from the wind. All the curls had come out. It looked like Silly String.

Then my head hit the glass, hard, and there was a hand on my arm. The shock made me stay quiet. My first thought was Ray. I wondered why he was so pissed he wanted to hurt me. But the voice was different. That's when I knew I was in trouble. My vision swarmed. My arms were pinned behind my back, like I was under arrest. I said, *Get off of me.* He clapped his hand over my mouth. I spat into his palm, but he didn't notice.

'Relax,' he said. 'I'm not gonna hurt you.'

He marched me between the cars. I tried the limp noodle. It only made things easier for him. When I kicked his shin, he stopped and showed me a knife, like one you'd use to gut a fish. I knew I had to do what he wanted.

It was dark and he was mostly dragging me, but once we passed under a floodlight and I saw his face in a flash. He wasn't anyone I'd ever seen before. His skin was pink, almost translucent, and he had eyes that reminded me of John Lennon's, with heavy lids. His face was covered in sores, like Ray's brother's when he was addicted to crystal meth. The next day they sat me down with a lady cop and she tried to help me make a picture of his face with a computer, but my memory didn't work the way I thought it would. The face in the drawing looked like every bad man.

I saw the tall sloping letters that said FOLEY FIELD ATHLETIC STADIUM. We'd come as far as the bleachers by the football field. He shoved me against the concrete. I felt the weight of him at my back, his hands prising my legs apart. I felt so sorry for Pop, since this was the last thing any daddy'd ever want to happen to his little girl, and since he'd been telling me to keep myself safe since I was old enough to understand the words.

He was hurting me. He kept telling me to shut up, but I was

sure it was him making the noise. I waited for him to finish. There was a pain like gunfire in my body, but my mind went someplace else. I was at the canyon smoking weed with Delaney. I was crossing the field by the school. I was floating on Morgan Lake. There was no pollution.

There's this dream I have where I'm older and I'm living someplace new. I have a job. I wear cloppy heels and a silk shirt. Maybe my job is something to do with helping people, like the lawyers on TV who represent the public. I drive home to visit Pop and no one recognises me. I drive by my high school and the gas station and the Sonic Drive-In, and Ray and Mr Murphy and Mrs Vasquez all look up to see who's driving that car down West Broadway. I'm so old and I've gathered so much power that it's like a disguise. No one can touch me through it. No one even recognises me but Pop and Luther. They're waiting for me on the front lawn.

We sit down to eat dinner together. They'll tell me they're glad to see me. They'll say they're happy I made something of myself.

PEAKS

Gideon came to pick me up from the train station in Sheffield. He was standing by the kiosk holding his phone. I had the upper hand of the person who sees first. He hadn't changed. Same curly dark head, greying at the temples since I'd known him; same unfashionable wire-rimmed glasses. Same posture: he had the faux-casual stance of the lanky man who was bullied as a child. I had the uncharitable thought that he could do with some sunlight. He waved when he saw me.

'I didn't know if I'd recognise you!' he said. I almost said, *Why, what did you expect*, but there was no sense starting a fight this early on. He held me at arm's length to appraise me, the way everyone seemed to do at that time in my life. He took my suitcase.

'You travel light,' he said. 'Maybe you can teach Yoni.'

'She has to take all the kids' stuff,' I said. 'It must be hard, travelling with them.' He glanced at me sideways as he shut the boot of the Fiat Punto.

Gideon is the only person who makes me defensive of my sister.

The children met us at the door. I heard their feet on the carpet, their whispers. When Gideon bent to flip open the letter slot, a pair of brown eyes blinked back, startled.

'They've been waiting all day,' he said.

'They need to lower their expectations,' I said, but it was too late: the door swung wide and the two girls stood there with identical expressions, part guilt, part ecstasy. They both yelled, *Daddy!* and hurled themselves at him, staring at me the whole time. He picked up the youngest. She fit herself against his shoulder, looking at me from beneath a choppy fringe.

'Aren't you going to say hello to your auntie?'

I knelt and the oldest obediently presented her cheek for a kiss.

'It's okay,' I said, 'we haven't seen each other for a long time. Do you remember when you came to Australia?'

She stared.

'I remember,' Gideon said. 'Travelling to the antipodes with a six-month-old and an almost-three-year-old. I remember far too well.'

'Mum said she was sick,' Mila said.

'Excuse me,' said Gideon. 'She is the cat's mother.'

'It's okay,' I said again. 'I was sick, but I'm better now. And, anyway, it's one you can't catch. I promise.'

'It was the same sick as Nan,' Mila said. 'Mum told me.'

'It was in a different part,' I said.

Then my sister appeared, wiping her hands on a tea towel. She was smiling as if she hadn't expected me at all, with her mouth wide open and an *ah-h-h-h* sound coming from her throat. She'd tossed the towel over one shoulder. When she hugged me, my face was pressed to the linen and I breathed in strong things—dirty dishwater and onion and fennel and a sour smell I couldn't name—and I was momentarily repulsed. I turned my nose to her neck like a lover instead. She began to stroke my hair. When we separated, I saw the girls and Gideon watching. All three of them had the same polite, unsteady smile. At last Yoni touched Gideon's arm.

'Could you do their bath? Dinner's still half an hour away.'

My sister seemed to have forgotten I'd never been in this house before. When Gideon thumped upstairs to bathe the girls, we left my suitcase in the hall by the door. It looked like I was ready for a midnight escape. I followed Yoni to the kitchen. I sat at the table and she took up grating a hunk of cheese.

'Can I do anything?'

'No. Just sit there. The girls have already eaten. It won't be far away.'

'Is that a Gideon thing?'

'What?'

'Feeding the girls first.'

She glanced at me over her shoulder. 'No. I don't know. We've always done it. Gives us time to talk at the end of the day. It's good to be able to eat at leisure.' She set a chopping board in front of me, then the grater and the cheese. 'Can you finish this? I need to do the salad.'

When we were children, living at the edges of Melbourne, it was Yoni, me, Mum and Dad around the dinner table every night, and there was no reason to eat anywhere else. I remember Yoni trying to convince Mum to let her eat tea in her room once, when she was studying for her HSC and couldn't afford the time to socialise or ask anyone else about their day. Mum went through the roof. Dad worked nights at the casino and slept through most of the day. Dinners were when we found out about each other.

I began to grate the cheese.

'How was London?' she asked.

'It was all right. I think I expected it to be the same as when I was backpacking.'

'What, when you were twenty-three?' Yoni turned to the sink to wash the spinach. I started to explain it, how I'd suddenly felt unsure of what to do or how to fill my days, how I'd gone to bed in my tiny hotel room at nine-thirty every night, lonely and full of dread, but I couldn't tell whether she was listening.

'Anyway,' I finished, 'it's good to finally be here with *you*.'

'We don't like London much,' Gideon said from the doorway. He poured three glasses of wine. I stood to match the two of them. The three of us were very close. It felt like a suicide pact.

'Cheers,' Yoni said, raising her glass. She held it between her fingers at the bottom of the stem. Mostly likely someone had told her to do it at a wine tasting once.

'What do the French say? To your health,' Gideon said. '*À votre santé.*'

The spare room was on the third floor, up a steep flight of stairs.

'Be careful if you come down to the loo in the night,' Gideon said.

'Have you ever tripped?' I asked.

'I did,' Yoni said, 'when we first moved in. I wasn't even drinking. I just slipped, went straight down. Bruised my coccyx.'

The three of us stood in the doorway saying a long goodnight. Gideon and Yoni pointed out everything I might possibly need, from the towel folded at the end of the bed to the internet access code to the wall heater to the windows set into the sloping roof, which could be opened by standing on a chair. When they'd said

goodnight for the last time, I lay on the quilt in my clothes.
I looked at the small dark squares of sky above me, one at either
end of the room. There was a streetlamp right outside the house.
I couldn't see it from the bed, but it flooded the room. When
I turned back the bed, the sheets were streaked with sordid
yellow shadows.

The room filled with pale light by five in the morning. It was
useless trying to sleep. I drank a cup of coffee in bed. I went back
to my book, the one I hadn't been able to concentrate on the day
before, sitting on the train. I was still reading when Mila, the oldest
of the girls, appeared in the doorway. She was wearing a floor-
length nightie speckled with tiny pink flowers. It made her look
oddly elderly.

'What are you doing?' she asked.

'Reading my book.'

'What book?'

'It's lots of short stories,' I said, 'mostly about sad men.'

'Why are you reading about sad men?'

'I don't know why. I think I might stop.'

It was one of those fashionable recommended books I'd bought
to take away with me. I like reading, but I get most of my books
from other people or from the recently returned shelf at the library.
When I have to choose my own, I feel overwhelmed. Suddenly
I don't trust my own taste and I buy something with a metallic
sticker on the front. This is also how I choose wine when I need
to spend more than ten dollars.

'Can I get in with you?' Mila asked.

I turned back the duvet. 'Of course you can.'

She climbed in beside me. I almost held out an arm for her, the
way I'd seen my sister do, but it would have felt strange. The last

time I'd seen Mila, she'd been in nappies. She was six now. We were strangers. She burrowed in deep, clutching the blanket to her face. I felt one chilly foot brush against my leg. Her eyes flashed at me in apology.

'Did you have any dreams?' I asked.

'One about a fire,' she said, 'but I knew it wasn't real because Daddy wasn't upset. If it was a real fire he'd yell, *Quick, quick, get out of the house.*' She still had the duvet over her nose and mouth. Her voice was muffled. Her accent had a weird lilt to it, nothing that matched either Gideon or Yoni.

'Do you have school today?' I asked.

'Yes.'

'Do you walk?'

'Yes. Or sometimes Mum drives me if it's raining.' She pulled the sheet back from her face, breathed in. 'You have a different smell to Mum.'

'All bodies smell a bit different,' I said.

'Why?'

'Oh—different chemicals and things, I suppose.' I thought of how surprised Yoni would be if she came in and saw the two of us. I thought of how our mother would have loved the girls.

After that Mila came to my room every day. I was usually awake when her face appeared at the top of the stairs, except for once, when she climbed in beside me without speaking. I couldn't tug myself out of sleep. I'm not sure how long she was there for, but when I woke up properly she was waiting with the sheet over her head. I saw the star shapes of her hands through the cotton.

Their kitchen was chaotic in the mornings. I preferred to stay out of the way, either in the yard if it were sunny, or upstairs reading while Gideon tore around the place and Yoni hurried the girls to get ready. She worked a few days a week, a receptionist job at a walk-in clinic, but she'd taken time off while I visited. I couldn't imagine the mornings when she was working, too. The noise was maddening; the constant scraping of chairs on the slate tiles in the kitchen, Yoni counting down the time to departure, shouting *Ten minutes* then *Five* up the stairs.

After she'd taken Mila to school, Yoni and I went for a walk in the valley. We had to drive down there, she explained, because Poppy would never make the hike back up the hilly streets. She zipped Poppy into a windbreaker, sat her on the carpeted stair to put on her socks and boots.

'It's not even that cold,' I said. 'She'll roast once we get moving.'

'The weather changes like that,' Yoni said, snapping her fingers. 'Like Melbourne. Anyway, nobody moves fast enough to get warm with a three-year-old.'

The sign at the entrance said EASY-GOING TRAIL. Before we'd properly started we passed a playground with a severe-looking metal slide set into a grassy slope. Poppy tugged on her mother's hand and asked if she could play.

'One slide,' Yoni said, 'then you can have a proper play on the way back.' We watched her toddler legs cross the playground.

'She can have a go now, can't she?' I asked. 'We're not in a hurry.'

'She'll be too knackered to walk if I let her play now,' Yoni said. 'Oh. I haven't said *knackered* in ages. It must be hearing you say it.'

'It looks painful,' I said. 'That slide—that bit at the end. Looks like it'd give you a jolt.'

We watched her watching the other children, fingers in her mouth, until it was her turn. From the top of the slide she glanced up to check we were looking. We waved. The angle at the base was so sharp I was sure she'd cry out. I waited for disaster, but she landed on two feet, rhapsodic. My sister knelt with her arms out-stretched. Poppy came running.

We walked the dense trail that followed the stream. Yoni stopped once in a while to point out old grinding stones to me, herons to Poppy. The three of us stood on an old stone bridge to examine the ducklings in the stream below. I'd expected Poppy to whinge, but she was a good, stoic walker. When at last she fell against Yoni and announced, *My legs are tired*, we turned back again. She ran on ahead anyway, singing to herself in a fuck-you sort of a way that made me love her and see her as a small person for the first time.

'I like your hair like that,' Yoni said.

'I didn't have much choice,' I said. It had grown back in dark and curly tufts, uneven at first, and my eyebrows coarse. I'd kept wearing woollen hats for a long time, which made me realise I was vain, after all.

'It suits you,' she said. 'Even the grey suits you. You look like a middle-aged actress in a French film.'

'Am I fucking the swim instructor? Or am I on a train contemplating suicide because my husband is fucking the swim instructor?'

'God, you're so difficult,' Yoni said. It was very easy to make her laugh. We were back at the start of the trail, the place where the world was marked EASY-GOING.

A few days, Yoni and I drove out to small towns, only thirty or forty minutes from where they lived. High Bradfield, Castleton, Hathersage. They were like something from the bucolic Friday-night English murder mysteries our mother loved. I wished she'd had a chance to see the absurd green of it all, the lambs, the crumbling stone, the wisteria hanging from the awnings of the old pubs. I said dumbly, over and over again, that it was like a postcard.

Yoni tilted her head as if looking at an abstract painting and said, *I suppose I've stopped seeing it like that.*

'It's funny—Yoni sounds more Australian when she's talking to you,' Gideon said one evening. We'd just finished dinner.

'I think you sound almost completely English,' I said to her.

'It wasn't really conscious. I still don't sound like I'm from Sheffield.'

'You don't sound like you're from the north at all,' Gideon said.

'I guess I sound more like you,' Yoni said.

'You're not really English, though,' Gideon said. 'You don't have that British bashfulness.'

Yoni rolled her eyes. '*Everything* embarrasses you.'

Gideon turned to me. 'Last week we were at the fish-and-chip shop and the woman was wrapping up our stuff and she went to put it into a plastic bag. And Yoni literally took the package from her and said, *We don't need the bag.*' He spread his hands. I realised the punchline had come and gone.

'They're bad for the environment,' Yoni said.

'I was *mortified*,' Gideon said.

'We had a fight about it outside the shop,' Yoni said.

I couldn't think of a thing to say. I reached for Gideon's and Yoni's plates, all crusts, congealed sauce and picked bones. I carried them to the kitchen. I looked through the window while the sink filled. The last of the day's sunlight fell across the climbing rose. It refracted from the garden hothouse in prisms of gold. The garden was pretty by accident, not through care. Yoni was hopeless with plants. Weeds sprouted between the pavers, and there were patches of disturbed earth from her failed attempts at various flowers.

I was almost finished with the dishes when she came to stand beside me. She picked up the tea towel and began to dry the plates in a dreamy way.

'I know you hate it when he talks like that,' she said.

'Yes.'

'I'm not going to defend him to you.'

'I don't want you to. I am very grateful to you both for having me. I know how much you love him,' I said. 'It's okay.'

'It is okay,' she said. We were both looking at the hothouse, both blinded by the glare.

We went into town. It rained. The bus windows were clouded with condensation, and Poppy drew wonky hearts with her fingers. We had coffee with a few of Yoni's friends. They were pleasant women. They laughed at small things. They pierced juice boxes with straws and passed them to waiting hands, stroked hair from foreheads, unzipped parkas without taking their eyes from each other as they spoke. My favourite was a Glaswegian woman. She worked as a sex-education officer at the university. When her little boy tugged at her shirt and began to chant, *Mummy mummy mummy*, she closed her hand over his, but did not turn from me. The message passed between them: the kid quietened instantly. It was so potent I almost forgot what I was saying. It was their signal, she explained when he was out of earshot. *He knows I've heard him, but he also knows he'd better not bloody interrupt me.*

Afterwards we walked across town, Poppy asleep in her stroller, to the winter garden. I'd expected a nineteenth-century hothouse, but it was a modern building, its ceiling made of elegant timber arches.

There was a group of schoolchildren, all in yellow hi-vis vests, clustered together eating lunch under the eye of their teacher. Their voices echoed in the space. I told Yoni about Gillian's hand signal.

'She's clever, isn't she,' Yoni said.

'It's another language just for them,' I said. The rain had started again, hard. I could see it smearing the ceiling of the glasshouse over the great palm leaves. 'When they were all asking me if I had children—'

'I'm sorry about that,' Yoni looked destroyed. 'You were very gracious.'

'No—I didn't care. But it would have made everyone uncomfortable if I'd said, *Oh, I can't have them now but it's all right.*'

'You *could* have them,' she said uncertainly. 'You have options.'

'If I'd said *I don't want them*, then.'

'I think illness frightens people,' she said.

'I am forty-two years old,' I said.

In the adjoining Millennium Gallery there was a John Ruskin exhibition. I'd never heard of him, but the plaques told me he was a Victorian writer who'd created a museum especially for the workers, to bring them *culture*. It was open in the evenings and on Sundays to allow the workers time to view the collection. Ruskin stipulated that the objects—the etchings, sculptures, poems, mosaics, paintings—be few and carefully selected so as to not overwhelm or bore the workers. Poppy was still asleep. Yoni and I were a long time moving around the room. We whispered to each other in a kind of truce. We stood before a display of minerals and I told her what I remembered about them.

'What about lapis lazuli?' she asked.

'It's supposed to have powerful healing energy. Enhances memory and learning abilities. Balances the energies of the throat chakra, blah, blah.'

I looked at our reflection in the glass case. Her arms were crossed, her brow tight. 'What if it's bullshit?'

'Well, it probably is,' I said. We looked at each other. We began to laugh.

• • •

By Sunday, my last day, the children had come down with head colds. Yoni and Gideon were terrified they'd pass it on to me, even though I kept telling them I was all better, I'd been better for months, and how could I have travelled for thirty hours on a plane if I was worried about germs. Yoni was also bitter about the weather. The sky was dark and heaving.

'We were supposed to go out to the Peaks,' she said, sounding crushed.

'We can still go,' I said.

'Look at the sky.'

'The worst that'll happen is we'll get wet,' I said. 'It's not really cold.'

'How about if I look after the girls and you two just go,' Gideon said.

Yoni looked doubtfully at Mila's dripping nose. She glanced at me.

'Come on,' I said. 'Let's go.'

We stopped for Irish coffee on the way.

'We should have done this the other way around,' Yoni said. 'We'll need something to warm up afterwards.'

'We can get another one,' I said. We were sitting in the window of an old pub. Its panes were brown and distorted with age, framed with lace curtains. Yoni propped her chin in her palm, smiled. She looked very tired. There were pennies stuffed into the hollows of the roof beams. When I pointed them out she went, *Oh, yeah* in a toneless voice. Walking back to the car we passed a bakery.

'Look,' I said, squinting in, 'the Ruskin loaf. He's everywhere.'

'Mm, there's a bakery around the corner from home does one the same. It's Gid's favourite. He loves Ruskin.'

'I bet he does,' I said nastily without knowing what I meant by it.

'You can't not trust him because he went to university,' Yoni said.

'Don't be ridiculous.'

'Because he *teaches* at a university, then.'

'It's nothing to do with that,' I said. 'You or I could have gone to university. We have HECS.'

'It's called something else now,' she said. She unlocked the car. 'Anyway, you were looking after Mum. You couldn't even consider it.'

When I finished school I worked in a café for a couple of years, then a bicycle repair shop. I went to TAFE and studied drafting. I did that for a while. Then I worked at a holistic healing practice. That was where the crystals came in. I only ever took bookings, but my boss liked me to know what I was talking about. I got another certificate and worked at a respite-care facility for intellectually disabled adults out in Warrnambool. I was living with a bloke there. When we split up I moved back to the city and never looked for another job in care. Our mother used to say, *You only ever stick with anything long enough to get good at it.* If she was right, I didn't really see the problem with it.

'I've got nothing against Gideon,' I said.

Yoni turned the key in the ignition. 'You're like a reverse snob.'

We didn't speak the whole way to the Peaks trail, or while we walked. It was not far, nor very steep. I kept turning to look at the view. We were higher up than I'd thought. The wind was powerful. I zipped my jacket over my lips.

'That's a concrete factory,' Yoni said, pointing to a greyish, hulking building in the distance. 'Sort of spoils the view.' It was so windy we were standing with our legs spread, knees bent, bracing ourselves. The green rolled on forever. Blurry horizon: it was already raining on the distant hills. I leaped up in the air and landed a foot from where I'd jumped.

'What are you doing?' Yoni said.

'The wind is so strong that it actually pushes you backwards. Do it.'

She hesitated, then jumped. Her hair whipped across her face, loose from its plait. She hitched her leggings up around her crotch. 'These are too big,' she said, 'and when they start to slide down I can feel the wind around my vag.' She laughed and I did, too. My nose and eyes were streaming.

I walked out across the cliff, half-rock, half-grass, to where the ground fell away. I stood a few feet back from the edge. I looked down at the concrete factory, at the cartography of the dry stone walls and unpaved roads.

'Don't go any further,' Yoni called. 'You're scaring me.'

I turned to walk back to her, to the safety of the plateau's centre. I held out my arms and leaned into the wind. It buffeted my whole body, puffed up my windbreaker. I felt as if I were floating. 'Do it,' I said. She had that same uncertain expression on her face.

'Yoni,' I said. 'Put your arms out.'

She came to stand beside me in the crucifixion pose.

'It's like flying,' she said. She was breathless. I could hear voices coming up the trail, carried on the turbulent air, but for a moment it was just the two of us in the whole world.

ETERNAL FATHER

At the end of my shift I put on a fresh pot of coffee and have a cup with JJ. We always do when we work together. He's my favourite of the cooks. Today he tells me a story about his granddaughter. Last week it was her third birthday. He phoned her in the morning. *She was confused*, he says. *She kept saying, 'But Poppy, where did my two go?'* He chuckles when he says it and I can tell he really loves her.

It's one of those mornings when the day doesn't ever really break. More snow coming. It's almost eight-thirty, but the sky is low and leaden. It makes the world feel small. The roads haven't been salted yet.

At home the red light on my answering machine is winking. I am the only person I know who still has one. But cell reception is patchy around here, and the tiny tapes remind me of when I was small. Mom and I would record a new greeting message every year.

It's Deenie on the machine. There's a show in Elizabethton tonight. *It'll be fun,* she says, *promise. The two of us could use a little circuit-breaker right now. I'll come pick you up so you don't have to drive.* My place is out of her way. She must really want a friend.

I met Deenie working at a titty bar in Johnson City. I hadn't been there long when she got into money trouble with the owner. Then she found out how old I was. It took her about three days to find us both another job at an all-night café in Elizabethton. They were only looking for one waitress but she convinced them to take us as a package deal. We still work there.

Deenie looks the way you want a waitress to look. She's five foot nothing, tiny, but round in the places that matter. All her features are exaggerated—huge hazel eyes, full lips, big teeth, mass of dark hair that she puts up in a bun when she's at work. Her little boy died of crib death. It happened right before I met her, but it was a long time before she told me. Sometimes in the night she wakes up and his face is pressed up against hers. She says it's the most terrifying feeling in the world. She's paralysed when it happens. She got his name tattooed in curly letters under one tit. One of the cooks, Lenny, is crazy about her, but she always says, *I don't shit where I eat.* I think she's smart.

I tell Deenie's voicemail I'll come to the show. I eat a spoonful of peanut butter and half an apple. Then I put on my long johns and boots and drive to Carver's Gap. The parking lot is empty. I stuff my thermos, crampons and headlamp in my pack and cross the road to the trailhead.

I never started hiking until I lived here. There are a ton of trails out this way, and a lot of people come to see the rhododendron garden in the spring. This time of year their leaves are iced over, and sometimes I can walk for hours and not see another soul.

It's funny how there are certain things you learn about yourself pretty late. Like, I'd never thought of myself as being a person who enjoys the outdoors, but it turns out I am.

I like all weather. The light out here in winter is one of the cleanest, most peaceful things I know. In the spruce forest by the trailhead it's bluish, spiked with gold when it's sunny. The world is silent when I'm walking through that balsam. Out on the balds it's quiet, too, but windier, and it's me, too, my body, making noise; the silvery sliding of my waterproofed limbs, my boots on the snow, my steady breath. The snow and ice make for hard work. By the time I reach Engine Gap, my calves are on fire. One time JJ drew me a diagram of lactic acid and how it works. I don't know how he knows about that stuff, but I always think of it when I'm hiking.

This part of the Appalachian trail switchbacks across the Tennessee–North Carolina state line. I like it for that, though maybe not everyone would care. When I was a kid I thought I'd never leave Louisiana. Then we did leave, after Katrina, but it was just the same in Florida. My mom had this way of making every place feel suffocating. In my eighth-grade geography classroom I used to stare at the map tacked to the wall. Our state flower was the orange blossom, our animal the Florida panther. Gainesville was marked with a blue star. It seemed impossibly distant from any borders. It turned out to be not so far. It was a sleep on a bus. That summer I was fifteen.

Here are some reasons why I like hiking: it encourages you to look for signs and signals, and also to make your own. There are obvious ones like blazes and cairns and tape, but if you want to pay attention it's easy to see where things have changed in small ways—a bit of your own jumper lint caught on a branch, animal tracks in dirt, and so on. Sometimes other hikers leave you messages, too. A branch over something that looks like a trail, but is actually a dry creek bed—they're telling you not to go that way. And I never sign them, but I like to read the guest books that some shelters have, and see other people's drawings and notes.

It teaches you to be prepared. I don't think you need hiking sticks or those ridiculous water bladders or packs the rich tourists carry, but I always take extra snacks and flares and my headlamp. I have a reflective blanket that folds down real small, a knife, things like that. Nothing bad has ever happened to me, but you have to take at least a little care. You'd be surprised how dumb people can be.

Today there's a cold disturbance in the air. The mountains are disappearing in cloud cover. The kind of weather that looks ugly in a city. I walk as far as the barn at Yellow Mountain Gap and drink my coffee sitting at the picnic table. The air freezes the coffee droplets at the lip of my thermos, the sweat on the back of my neck, the damp hair at my temples. I try to pee, but my body won't work in the cold. I watch the billowing sky, squatted, with my ass to the snow. Mist rolling in over Roaring Creek. Time to turn back.

Last time I saw Carson he showed me a catalogue. He'd circled a watch, one of those fancy outdoor ones with a compass and a GPS. It could tell you how high up you were. It was chunky and black. He said, *How would you like something like that for Christmas?* I had to find a gentle way to tell him it was too much for him to buy, too much for me to accept. Too heavy a thing for us.

By the time I make it back to the car, it's near dark. At home I strip off all my layers and take a Xanax. I run the bath as hot as I can stand. The shampoo's frozen. I lie in the tub with the bottle between my thighs. Knuckly red chilblains are blooming across my fingers. I should have warmed up gradually. My problem is that I've never had much patience for discomfort.

Deenie comes by after seven. I open the door to her jiggling up and down to keep warm. She's wearing a puffy jacket and tight jeans and boots with a little heel. She has butterfly clips in her hair. She fixes her eyeliner in front of the speckled hall mirror while I check all the lights and slide a hot water bottle under my quilt for later.

'Is Carson coming?' she asks as I lock up.

'I didn't ask him.'

'Why don't you call him now?'

Her car has reindeer antlers clipped to the windows and a stuffed red nose on the grill. The nose is spattered with mud.

'We didn't say we'd see each other this weekend,' I say.

She slides into the driver's seat, inspects her mouth in the rear-view mirror. 'You know that's weird, right? You know you're real weird about him?'

'I know.'

'You treat that boy right.' She does a mafia accent, waggling her finger at me.

The road's been ploughed since the morning, but it's still a mess.

'Why don't you keep in a low gear,' I say.

'Will you chill out?' she says. 'I'm a good driver.'

'I know you are. Anyone could lose control here.'

'Listen. Anyone could die any time of day.'

Deenie says stuff like that when she means to make me feel better. Lately she's been all up in my ass about yoga. I'm twenty-two, and she's only four years older, but she likes to pull that shit sometimes because I don't have a mom anymore and she's not one anymore. She's like, *Quit worrying so much and then you won't need those damn pills*, but since she doesn't ever get so afraid she can't leave her room, it's hard to take her serious. There are a lot of things I'm scared of, and I know it makes me hard to get along with at times. Some of the big ones are: needles. Swimming pool filters. Waking up in the night and seeing someone standing in the room watching me. Being buried alive. Pictures of Jim Jones where he's wearing those creepy glasses. Cancer. Airplanes. Strangers. Hurricanes. Driving in bad weather, especially at night.

'So anyways,' she's saying, and I realise I haven't been listening. 'Galileo dumped his daughters in a convent. You used to be able to do that when they were teenagers, but I mean they were real young.'

She's taking the corners too fast. I think she's talking about her niece's school play. I remember she was going to see it the other night.

'That is young,' I say.

Deenie's eyes slide towards me. 'You still thinking about this fucking road.'

'I can't believe they still didn't salt it.'

'Jesus,' she says. 'You forget to take your pill today, or what?' but I feel her slow down infinitesimally. We pass the turn-off for the RV park at Sugar Hollow.

'What'd you do today, anyway?' she asks.

'My shift finished at eight. I came home and went for a walk.'

'A hike?'

'Yeah. I started at Carver's Gap.'

'How far did you go?'

'Like six hours maybe,' I say. The names don't mean anything to her.

She whistles. 'You must have done something real bad in a past life that you feel like you gotta punish your body like that.'

'It's not like that.'

'How's it like, then?'

'It doesn't hurt.'

'Well, it sure sounds like it.'

Her radio is playing shitty pop but she's got it turned down low. Neither of us says anything until we reach the intersection of the 19E.

'You should tell Carson to come tonight,' she says. She's gentle but I can decode what she means: *I want us to have a good night but I'm scared you'll freak out and I'll be too drunk to look after you properly but someone should.*

She hands me her cell. I've got that greasy feeling in my gut. I don't want to give the wrong idea about Carson. He's a good guy. He loves his little girl. I haven't met her yet, but that's on me. He says he thinks we'd like each other. Haleigh is six. She lives with her mom most of the time, but Carson puts in a lot with her. He's always picking her up from school and taking her places. He sometimes apologises, says, *Sorry I can't tonight, I got Haleigh*, but he says it in a way that I know is not negotiable, and I like that. His little girl ought to come before me.

Some other things: he has a job driving oil tankers. His knuckles spell out FUCK CARS because he used to be a motorcycle mechanic. He bought me a pair of real hiking boots. When he was fourteen, he got arrested for stealing copper wiring. When he was sixteen, he got caught breaking into the mausoleum and stealing gold fillings from skulls. That's the sort of thing that'd freak Deenie out, but I can understand it. Hunger makes you forget grace.

My fingers find the pattern of his number. He doesn't pick up, and I'm spared.

The warm-up band is shitty, and the second warm-up band's not much better. In fact, two of the same guys play in both, which probably explains why. We crack jokes for a while, but it's hard to hear over the caterwauling on the stage.

At some point Deenie disappears. When I look around I see her standing by the bar talking to a stranger. He's wearing a denim jacket lined with fleece and she's sucking her drink through a straw and standing on one hip and I know what it adds up to and it makes me tired for her, even though I know she likes it. I spot a free booth and slide in across the sticky seats. I weigh the mass of what's around me. Room edged with bodies, dull whine of over-drive guitars that makes me think of bees. I finish my drink and roll the ice cubes in my mouth.

'You mind if I sit here?' I see his figure looming at the edge of my vision.

'Go ahead,' I say, but I keep my eyes fixed on the stage, pretending I'm watching the band.

'You here alone?' he asks.

I shake my head. 'My friend's'—I drag my hand through the air—'around someplace.'

He smiles. 'I'm Rudy.'

'Nice to meet you, Rudy.'

'Are you into this?' he asks, jerking his thumb towards the stage.

I shrug. I go to sip my drink and remember it's all gone. I look around for Deenie.

'You're a tough nut, huh?' Rudy says. 'Whatsamatter—you don't like men?'

The band finishes. At last I spot Deenie by the bar. She's alone again, holding our coats, waving at me to leave.

'I'm going now,' I say.

I find Deenie waiting by the door. It's snowing again, big wet flakes the size of a dime that slide down the back of my neck while I zip my jacket.

'Who was that?'

'His name was Rudy.' I don't look at her because I know she'll be wearing that face of *you're-so-weird*. I'm shivering.

'You want to go someplace else?' she says. 'The band's done. Thank Christ.'

'See, this is what I don't understand about going out,' I say. 'You never just enjoy the one place. You end up running around chasing shit all night, only there's never anything worth chasing.'

'I thought they were gonna be good,' she shrugs.

I like how Deenie doesn't apologise for shit that's not her fault.

She unwraps us each a stick of gum. She starts saying the names of bars until I'm like, *You choose*. We link arms and walk that way until we have to break apart to avoid some ice on the pavement.

'What about your guy,' I say.

'What guy?'

'The cowboy in the fleece jacket.'

'I gave him my cell. He can call if he wants to.'

'He'll call.'

'Maybe,' she says.

We're standing in front of the bar. The windows are so fogged I can't see anything inside but blurry shadows crossing lights. Deenie pushes open the door and stands aside.

'Go on,' she says. 'First one's on me.'

When Deenie's drunk she gets this cloudy look. Hazy eyes. We stand side by side in the restrooms and I watch her redo her makeup. Powder to make her skin light up, silver dust under her eyes, slicks of black on the lids. When she fucks up one eye she says, *Oh shit, can you pass me some TP real quick?* If Deenie's the waitress who makes you look twice, I'm the one you don't notice.

It's funny, 'cause I'm a head taller than her. And we have similar hair—dark, and lots of it. But I'm straight-hipped where she's round, plain where she's long lashes and dimples, papery-skinned where she's golden. I don't mind that. I like to be not noticed. My legs have mountain muscle.

The bathroom door swings wide and we trip out, clutching at each other. Deenie stumbles into the cigarette machine. On the front is a perspex panel with a poster in it, lit from behind. It has a picture of two cowboys, and underneath it says *Come to Marlboro Country*. Deenie poses like one of the cowboys, tipping an invisible hat. She laughs. 'I'm so fucked up,' she says.

'Let's go.'

'Hold up.' She pulls me towards the bar. 'I think I saw Mike coming out of the men's before.'

Mike is a tattooist and also a hospital janitor, only he never seems to do either job. Whenever I see him, day or night, he's shooting pool or about to head off fishing or driving his buddy Shaun someplace. He comes into the restaurant a lot, all hours, but he's never on his way to or from work. I can't figure out him and Deenie. They're flirty, but in an easy way that makes me wonder if they didn't fuck a long time ago and never since.

Sure enough, he's standing by the dartboard watching a friend play. When he sees Deenie, though, he peels away from the game and the three of us sit at the bar. Deenie buys us shots.

'Where're you all going after this?' he asks.

'Home,' I say, and Deenie rolls her eyes.

'We got no plans,' she says. 'Hey, Mikey, what time do they close up at that tattoo place of yours tonight?'

'Eleven. How come?'

'I want one. She lifts her hair, touches the back of her neck. 'Here.'

'Not tonight, D.'

'C'mon,' she says. 'This is my first Saturday night off in a month, and the whole thing's been a bust. I need something to make it worthwhile.'

'You know what you want?'

'Yeah.'

'I won't do it if you're drunk.'

'I'm not.'

Mike doesn't believe her. We're all laughing.

'Ask her,' Deenie says, nodding towards me. 'I been talking about it a long time.'

'She has,' I confirm. I don't say that I think it's a dumb idea. What she wants is her little boy's date of birth in Roman numerals. I tried to tell her that people will ask what the numbers mean, and she's gonna have to talk about it, but she didn't see the problem. If my baby died, I would hate to have the conversation-starter on my skin, but what do I know.

Mike looks from my face to Deenie's.

'All right,' he says. 'But once it's inked, it's there forever.'

'I know that, dumbass, I already got three.'

Mike raises his eyebrows. I guess they haven't fucked yet.

'Let's go,' Deenie says. Mike stands up so fast his head brushes the fringe on the light hanging over the bar, and we all laugh fresh.

The tattoo parlour is closed. Mike makes a big show of sneaking in, shushing us. It's cold inside. He hits a switch and the whole place goes lightning-strike white. We quieten down. I hoist myself up onto a bench and sit with my knees tucked to my chest to keep warm.

Deenie fixes her hair in a bun, the way she wears it at work. Mike sits behind her, one leg either side of her chair. I can see a strip of dirty grey-white cotton where his jeans are sliding off his ass. He asks Deenie if she's comfortable. He shaves the back of her neck with a disposable razor the colour of a tangerine, then wipes it down with rubbing alcohol. I feel like I'm watching a minor medical procedure. I saw a kid get a spinal tap on a TV show once. From where I sit, Deenie could be having her blood drawn to discover some rare illness, some evil division of cells. I'm so deep in the fantasy that, for a second, I forget what's going on and where we really are. The tattoo gun hums and sighs. I keep expecting her to cry out, maybe reach for my hand, but her expression is dreamy and determined. I have a sudden flash of thought: that's how her face would have looked when she was giving birth. It feels like I'm watching something private, but I can't look away.

When he's all done, Mike holds up a mirror so Deenie can see it.

'You did a real good job.' Her voice sounds like she hasn't used it in weeks. 'Thanks, Mike.'

He fixes a bandage over the numbers. Deenie swings her legs around so she's facing us both. She presses her hands together and wedges them between her thighs. She shivers.

'Oh. I just got cold all of a sudden. And I feel *one hundred per cent* sober again.' She smiles.

Mike finds three beers in the back and we drink them fast, Deenie still on the chair that reminds me of the dentist. She and Mike swap stories, though it's mostly Mike talking. I try to laugh at the right moments but I'm still so on edge. We drink another beer. My mouth has that gluey stop-start taste.

'What do you want to do now?' Deenie asks at last.

Mike's knee is jiggling up and down. He scratches his ear. 'I've gonna go pick up some chalk for a friend,' he says. 'You wanna come? See if they got anything you want?'

'I don't do that shit,' Deenie says.

'I don't, either. They got other stuff, too. C'mon.'

Deenie looks at me with a challenge in her eyes. I don't say anything. And that's how we're in the back of Mike's car, flying down the highway again, a plastic bottle of Southern between my knees. The radio is staticky. I want to keep track of where we are. I put my forehead to the window. Streaming night. Gas station, church, high school, fields, pool hall, liquor store, billboard that reads TROUBLED? TRY PRAYER. I haven't been to church in a long time. In Gainesville I caught the bus every week. But Sunday mass here makes me feel like I'm being smothered. People notice if you skip a week. People notice if you don't want to hang around for chit-chat afterwards. It depletes me, that stuff. I think, if God exists, He would understand that.

I also think he probably doesn't care so much about the number of Hail Marys you say, or whether you are neglectful of your prayers. Those rituals are mostly for us, anyway. I think He's probably more concerned with how nice of a person you are. I think God's smart enough to work it out without us sucking up to him, but not everyone feels that way. For example: right after I moved here, I went to confession and told the priest about falling asleep during mass. Then I explained I fell asleep because I'd been working a lot of nights. Then I felt I should explain what I was doing. *I was working at Gussy's. You know that place, Father? You know what kind of place that is?* He did. I said I was sorry for it and all of my sins, and he gave me my penance, but I felt something in him shift. I don't think I imagined it. I am the sort of person who is comfortable examining her sins, and I don't mind telling the right person about them. But this priest was not the right person.

• • •

Mike pulls into a motel. It's a two-storey place with concrete stairs and ugly wrought-iron banisters, so old that the lit-up sign still says COLOR TELEVISION. Mike jumps out of the car to tap at number 11. The door swings open and a little weedy guy stands there, middle-aged, and kind of shrunk. He blinks, because Mike's left his headlights on and he's standing full in their glare. The two of them talk a while. The weedy guy looks like he would have been bullied in high school and probably all his life, but I can see Mike is asking him for something and he's not backing down. He lights a cigarette, squinting at Deenie and me through the windscreen. Mike gestures for us to come over. Deenie twists around in her seat to look at me.

'Do you have a bad feeling?' she asks.

I shrug.

'You always have a bad feeling,' she says, more or less to herself, and I hear the click of her seatbelt.

The guy ushers the three of us inside. It stinks like a teenage boy's bedroom. On the wall is a mural of Adam and Eve. It's a weird picture—they're fat child-humans, but not in a cherubic way. There's something grotesque about them. They stand in a rainforest of blues and greens, trees with figgy-looking leaves. A cartoon serpent is coiled behind them. He looks sad, as if he's sorry for what he's about to do.

Mike's staring at me like he's waiting for a response, but I don't know what the question was.

'Whatever. At this point, a dime,' Deenie says.

The guy adjusts his balls. 'Angel will have something,' he says. He knocks on the door adjoining the next room with his cigarette between his knuckles, smoked right down to the filter, and a woman opens it. Her big red tits and puddingy arms spill from her tank top. I look past her and see that there's a mural on her

126

wall, too, only it seems to be Moses among the cattails. She sees me looking. She smiles.

She and Deenie sit side by side on the bed like they're old friends, and I hang in the doorway between the two rooms.

'You want some too, honey?' Angel asks me, her medicine bag open on her thighs like a giant slack mouth.

I pull my sleeves down over my hands. 'You got any dexy?'

'I just might, you know,' she says. 'I just might.'

There's a scuffle next door, and when I turn Mike and the weedy guy are tussling. Neither of them is any good at it, and it's almost funny to see them slapping and pulling at each other.

'The fuck are they doing in there?' Deenie asks, craning her head to see what I can. Mike's a head taller, but the little guy's full of sudden rage. He's grunting like a pig. Mike pushes him against the mirror, and then into the plastic venetian blinds. They make a rippling sound.

'Would you quit it,' Deenie yells. There's a series of muffled thumps and some more snorting, and then an explosion. It's so loud the world goes white and silent. I realise I'm lying flat on the carpet on my belly, nose pressed to the ashy carpet, and for a moment I can't move. Mike's screaming, *Fuck! Fuck!* in a strange, high-pitched voice. Then Deenie's boots are moving past my face. She's stepping over me where I lie in the doorway, swearing, and I scramble to my feet. My blood's going too fast, as if it's going to split out of my limbs. The weedy guy is rolling around on the carpet like a beetle that can't right itself. Deenie's kneeling over him, pressing something to his thigh, and when she takes it away I see a dark flower on his jeans.

'Keep still, you *moron*,' she says, like she's talking to a jerk customer. 'I'm trying to help. It's not even that bad.' She looks up at me, at Mike. 'Anyone gonna call 911?'

'It's done, honey,' Angel calls from the other room.

'What did you say?' the guy says hoarsely.

'I said you shot yourself in the damn leg.'

Angel slams the door adjoining the rooms.

'I'm gonna beat feet,' Mike says.

The guy's stopped writhing around. 'I need a smoke,' he says. I find his cigarettes and light one for him. I take it out of my mouth and nudge it between his grey, peeling lips. He squints up at me. 'You been here all along?'

He's still smoking when they put him on a gurney, hairy liver-spotted hands poking out from yellowed cuffs. Deenie and I stand outside Angel's door in case someone needs to take a statement from us, but the EMTs come and go, and no police show up. It's snowing again. We go back into the guy's stinky room. Deenie washes her hands in the bathroom sink. The water drains away a brownish colour. I poke around his stuff and find a bottle of bourbon in his bedside drawer.

'Finders keepers,' Deenie says. There's nothing to mix it with so we take it in turns to swig, gag, wipe our mouths and pass the bottle. I try to remember where Deenie's parked. I realise we drove to the show and nowhere else since, and her car is still in the lot.

'Fuck *that*,' she says. 'Why did you have to think of that now?'

'How else are we going to get home.'

'Can't you call Carson to come get us?'

'It's 3 a.m. I'm not doing that.'

'Maybe Angel will help us out,' Deenie says, and we crack up.

In the bar fridge we find a couple cans of beer. We open one, stuff the rest in our jacket pockets and walk the four miles back into town. Most of it's highway, and every time a car passes we have to jump out of the way of a storm of gravel and ice bullets. Deenie is remarkably uncomplaining, when you take into account the little heel on her boots and the fact she hates walking. Still, though, we don't talk much. We pass the beer between us and drink it quickly because it's too cold to have our hands out of pockets.

I've told Deenie a lot of things. How, after Katrina, when we were allowed back into our house, the first thing Mom did was pin the flag on the living room wall. The water was still ankle-deep and everything smelled damp, of shit and mould. She sat on one of the kitchen chairs and I knew not to ask how we were going to fix things. How I saw Mrs Gregory's body by accident. Overheard one cop say to another that he never knew so many people couldn't swim. How I stole all my mom's emergency money just so I could leave her. How terrified I was when Deenie told me she'd got us a job at Virgil's, 'cause I was fifteen and could barely use a can-opener, let alone carry three plates at once. I've told her stuff about Florida. Not the small stuff, though. The fruit rotting under the trees; how the smell used to stick in my nose. Playing hooky to buy weed with the older kids. Singing 'Eternal Father', my favourite, O hear us when we cry to thee / For those in peril on the sea, at St Patrick's. People pulling into our drive at night to shoot up under the streetlight. The wall of the storage warehouse on NE 27th, where we used to write the names of people who died. The names of the neighbourhoods where we lived: Pine Park, Cedar Grove, Lamplighter. The confederate flag on Mom's boyfriend's car.

The bar's long closed, and Deenie's is the only car in the lot. We collapse in the front seat, clumsy with all our puffy layers and our frozen fingers. She starts the engine to blast the heater, and I tuck my knees to my chest. My ears are ringing.

'You're right about this tattoo,' she says. Her voice is quiet. 'Everyone and his bitch-ass brother is gonna ask what it means, and I'll have to keep telling them.'

'Does it hurt?'

'A little.' Her fingers skirt the square of bandage. The skin around it looks tender; the hair at the back of her neck is dark and downy.

'You know what would help?' she says. She reaches for the pocket behind the passenger seat and pulls out a sandwich baggie. It's a pathetic bud, but we smoke it anyway. She fiddles around until she finds the lever to lay her seat back. She closes her eyes.

'I don't know,' she says after a while. 'It's like it's been cut with meth.'

Maybe it's only because she said it, but I start feeling bad in the heart then. 'We have to get home,' I say.

'Let's just hang out here for a while.'

'It's fucking freezing. We can't stay here.'

'I don't mean all *night*. I'm not in a state to drive right now, okay?' She opens her eyes again, looks at me. 'Are you in a real bad place right now?'

I say nothing.

'We just have to ride this out,' she says.

My breath is coming faster and faster, but I can't get enough air in. The heater's too hot; there's too much touching me. I claw at the door handle but it won't open.

'What's wrong,' Deenie says. 'Calm down.'

I'm yanking at the door but my fingers won't work. They're frozen, they've turned to cement.

'It's broken. The lock is stuck,' she says. She opens her door and gets out, and I scramble across the console and fall to my knees gagging for the fresh air. Deenie's saying my name. Her face is everywhere. She takes off her puffy jacket and wraps it around me. It seems demented. Deenie's tiny and I'm not, and anyway I'm already bundled into my own coat. The extra layer is suffocating. But Deenie's arms are right around me, strong as any woman or machine, and she's saying, *We are here, we are here, we are here* like a prayer. I'm on all fours, my hands pressed to the icy gravel, and she's holding me together. I stop fighting her. I try to breathe in time with her words. My body slows down. I can see Deenie again. Just her face, just one of her. She's crouched, shivering. She's shivering because her jacket's still wrapped around me. Pieces of hair have frozen to the snot on my face. I sit back on my heels. The knees of my jeans are soaked through. My nails are all torn and bloodied. I shrug off her jacket and pass it back to her.

'You're meant to do that with dogs,' Deenie says. Breathless, smiling. 'Like, wrap them up real tight when they're scared. I read it one time.'

She is a good friend.

She presses her keys into my hand.

I don't know how long the drive home takes, but I sit on about ten miles most of the way. Deenie falls asleep and somehow that's better. It leaves me to concentrate on the road, not what she might be thinking about me. Once, on Roan Mountain Road, I have to stop altogether. I mean to pull over to the shoulder, but I can't bring myself to get any closer to the edge, the place where the earth falls away, so I just stop in the middle of the road. It's black ice, snow like a locust swarm on the windscreen. I hug myself and pretend it's Deenie's arms, like before; that I'm held real tight and safe. I count while I breathe. Then I can start again.

When we pull into my driveway at last, I jump out of the car to open the gate and leave the door open. It's the cold air that wakes her.

'Oh my lord,' she says. 'It's fucking *frigid*.' She yawns and looks at me. 'Hey. You did it. We're here.'

It feels like something's drained out of me. We stagger up the porch and through to the kitchen. My breath comes out in grey clouds. Deenie roots around in my cupboards, refrigerator, freezer, settles for a Pop-Tart. She doesn't even toast it, just eats it straight from the foil package. She squats on the floor like she's taking a shit. One hand holds the Pop-Tart, the other tucked under her armpit.

'You've got almost nothing,' she says.

'I have everything I need.'

'You don't got a bed.'

'I do. I have a mattress.'

The hot water bottle has cooled. I kick it on to the floor and pile on an extra quilt instead.

'Flannel sheets,' Deenie sighs.

When it gets light again I will get up and fix us scrambled eggs. Deenie won't eat any; she'll vomit watery yellow barf and lie in my bed all day. I will drive to Grandfather Mountain and do a walk—just long enough to sweat out the bad stuff—and stop for a coffee on my way home. Later in the afternoon I'll go to work, and JJ will tell me about something smart his granddaughter said, and Deenie will show up but she'll be useless and I'll have to do twice my own work. But for now, we're under the weight of so many blankets it's hard to move.

Too tired for sleep.

We play this game with hypotheticals. *What would you do if you got a thousand dollars tomorrow?* We mostly ask the same questions. We know each other's answers.

'If you could move anywhere,' Deenie says, 'where would you go?'

'Maybe Mexico. What about you?'

'Nueva York.'

'If you could do any job, what would you do?' I ask.

'I'd be an actress. You?'

'What's that job where you cut open bodies to work out how they died.'

'Oh, shit! Like that show *Autopsy*?'

'Yeah.'

'I wouldn't want to hang out with no dead people,' Deenie says.

'It'd be sort of like a puzzle.'

'What happened to being a nature photographer?' she asks, and we start to laugh. We're tired and maybe still high. It overwhelms us. My face aches with it, the absurdity of these new bright lives we invent for ourselves.

When we're quiet at last, she tucks her arms behind her head. 'I saw this French movie once,' she says, 'and the man's smoking, and the woman takes the cigarette out of his mouth, kisses him, then puts the cigarette back. I've always wanted to do that.'

She rolls over to face me, drapes her legs over mine.

'You have to go back to school to cut people open,' she says seriously.

'I know that. I only said it for the game.'

'Well, maybe you should go back to school for something.'

'I'm too tall for ninth grade now.'

She holds my face in her hands. I don't like her looking at me so close. She says, *Can't you think of one thing you want to do?* I try, but nothing comes into my head. I don't imagine working for Virgil forever, but there'd be worse things. He's been kind to me.

'Maybe you should have a baby,' Deenie says. 'Then you'd have something to focus on.'

A truck passes by outside. The headlights flash against the curtain.

'You're so weird,' she says. 'You'd rather spend a week on a mountain by yourself than talk to a stranger in a bar for five minutes.'

When the noise of the truck engine fades, the world is so quiet. I can hear Deenie's breathing, the catch of my toenail on the bedsheet, the tick of my eyelashes when I blink.

'I feel like I'm talking to myself,' Deenie says.

My blood beats. *By the time we're warm, we'll be asleep*, I think.

ALPINE ROAD

Mornings were when they were most forgiving of each other. When they fucked now it was first thing, while they were still kind.

Before Clive got sick, he was always up early. He worked at the power plant in Hazelwood. Even when he'd been on night shift, he'd get up and make the coffee.

These days he might not get out of bed at all. Mostly Franca woke when Billy wormed his way between their bodies, smelling of sleepy toddler. She'd lie there feeling his hot belly pressed against her back, his fingers in her hair. She'd go to the kitchen and do the kids' lunches, make the coffee. Clive'd be where she left him. Sometimes the blanket was too much for him to lift. He'd stopped saying *sorry* a long time ago.

He was having a good week. Franca heard him moving around the kitchen. The front door slapped shut. She sat up and looked through the blinds. There was frost on the lawn. Clive was barefoot, shirtless, carrying two plates of toast across the yard to the caravan, propped up on its bricks, where the older two slept. He banged on the metal with his fist. He shouted *Gendarmes!* It was a joke the kids wouldn't understand. The door swung open. Emily stood with a half-smile, wiping sleep from her face. Her mouth moved. Franca couldn't hear what she said, but it might have been *I knew it wasn't Mum.* Franca never brought them toast with jam in the mornings.

'There was a spider the size of a five-cent coin in the caravan,' Clive reported. He sat on the end of the bed. 'Kurt was carrying on the worst.'

'Thanks for getting them breakfast.'

Her shoulders were wet from the shower. The house was so cold she could see her breath.

'Listen, I'm getting Cate to pick up the kids from school today,' she said. 'There's a meeting about the bargaining agreement after work.'

'I can get them.'

She bunched her stockings at the ankles. 'It's okay. It's probably best to ask Cate. So we know for sure. You know. If you start to fade by then.'

He was gracious. He said nothing.

'I'll pick them up after five,' Franca said, 'then come and get you and Billy.'

'We still going to your parents' for tea?'

'Only if you're up to it. Otherwise I can just go with the kids.'

'I'll be right.' Clive scratched his ear. 'What'd you say it was at work?'

'The meeting for the bargaining agreement. I haven't been able to get to the others.'

'What's the go?'

'It's all still a bit over my head. I know they're talking about changing our pay from fortnightly to monthly.'

'Well, that wouldn't be the end of the world,' Clive said. 'We always work something out.'

Franca felt that sudden rage rolling in. 'Who does?'

'What?'

'*Who works it out*, I said.'

Clive looked at her steadily. Franca dropped her head.

She went to Billy's room. He was awake, one fist clenched at the corner of his sheepskin rug. He was two and a half and he'd had a name all along, but they still called him *the baby*. He sat up, beamed at her.

She made the lunches. She wiped the crumbs from the bench. The house needed restumping so badly that when she'd dropped the frozen peas last night, they'd rolled and collected in the corner of the kitchen by the door. The kids had crouched, pinching them between their fingers. Kurt said, *See, Mum, woulda been worse if the house wasn't falling down. At least they're all in the one spot.* He and Emily slept in the caravan because it was warmer than their bedroom with its rotted weatherboards, the hole under the window spewing damp Insulwool. They were good at making adventures of things.

Franca took the scraps out to the chooks. She stood by the caravan and tried to decode the conversation inside.

'Look! The sun fell!'

'Can you stop putting it in my face?'

She tapped on the door. 'Are you two showered? We're leaving in ten. Get a wriggle on.'

When she went back to the bedroom, the baby was in bed with Clive, in the curl of his arm. They had the same face.

137

'It's a real sickness,' Clive said. 'I'm really crook.'

Franca was helpless. She stood holding her coat. 'I never said you weren't.'

In the drawer beside his bed was a bible, a broken watch, his prescriptions and some foreign coins he kept to prove to himself he'd left the country. There were photos, too—mostly of the kids, but there was one picture of Franca from before they were married. She was naked, standing in front of a curtain. Shy pubic bone, one arm tucked behind her back politely. Franca didn't like the photo, or didn't see herself in it. She looked too much of a child. After the second baby she'd gone away, left him with the kids. When she came back Emily was eleven months old and didn't recognise her. Clive knew nothing about where she'd been or what she'd done that year. She didn't know if he'd ever trust her again.

Franca worked four days a week at the Latrobe Valley Magistrates' Court, all pale blue glass and clean angles. It had been built ten years ago, but she still thought of it as new. She was a stenographer. She liked the solemnity of the courts. She liked the drive to and from work. There was comfort in the skinny poplars, the long driveways, the husks of burnt-out cars in front yards, the gutted petrol station, the paddocks, the roadside signs to tiny cemeteries. This time of year, canola; fields of sunshine, the mountains. On Fridays she worked at Bairnsdale, closer to home. It was a smaller courthouse, set down by the brown river, two streets back from the grand brick building and the motels.

Clive hadn't worked in two years, but before, they could coordinate their lunch breaks some days. It was about ten minutes from the court to the power station. She'd meet him in the car park and they'd eat their sandwiches in the station wagon beneath the brutal concrete building, like something from the pages on the Eastern

Bloc in her high school atlas. It had eight towers, set in pairs, and red capital letters spelling out HAZELWOOD. When she'd been on mat leave, she'd sometimes taken the kids to the lake next door. Its water was used to cool the station.

It seemed like all the men in the valley worked there, or at the Yallourn plant, or else in the coalmine. Franca used to be reassured by its hulking brown shape on the horizon. You could see it from the highway for miles. In the right weather, you could see the plumes of shit it belched out into the atmosphere. Now when she saw it, it meant other people's husbands.

The end of the day was the wrong time for the meeting. Franca could barely follow. She'd been concentrating on voices and words all day. The union rep was a young man, impossibly articulate. He said things like, *There has not been a pay rise commensurate with the cost of living in five years. Waiting an additional year for that increase is problematic. I'm sure you understand.*

Franca wanted to ask the right questions but she was giddy. *Plenty of employers are going with monthly pays,* the IR lawyer was saying. *It's to do with compliance costs. Workers can adapt. It's the same amount of money.*

It's not the same, Franca thought, but the union guy was already saying it for her. *It seems punitive to move from two weeks to four when you know you're working with people already in a low-wage bracket, who already have to budget very carefully—*

Everyone was talking at once. The room was too full, too warm.

'Right,' someone said, 'we'll get the minutes out early next week. Anything else?'

'I just wanted to ask about carer's leave,' Franca said. The room of faces turned to her. 'I saw in the last transcript something about medical certificates.' Her hand hovered by her ear as if she were a schoolgirl with a question.

She drove past Stephen's on an impulse. His car was in the driveway. She tapped on the door and watched his figure approach through the bubble glass. He asked if she wanted coffee. She said, *I have to get the kids.* They fucked in a hurry. He held her wrists and pinned her down. His face hovered over her. His features blurred when he came. She thought, dimly, that there was something pathetic about the two of them, her thighs clenched around his hips.

Afterwards she fell asleep. It was only few minutes but she woke panicked, scrambled to sit up. His heavy arm fell away from her.

'Whassatime?'

'Ten past six.'

Franca lay down again, jackhammer heart.

'Have you been here the whole time?' she asked.

He stared at her. She felt foolish, dazed.

When she left the sky was paper-coloured. All the cows had started their journey home, their tender ears flattened. She parked out the front of Cate and Sonja's. No one answered when she knocked. She heard the high cuts of the kids' voices out in the yard. She pushed through the side gate.

'That baby, I mean, she had lead rings under her eyes,' Sonja was saying. 'They had to get out of the city.'

The two women were sitting on the deck, rugged up against the thin sun. They looked like royals surveying a kingdom: their sloping lot, the ashy grass, the kids kicking a footy at the bottom of the yard. Franca did a small wave.

'Hullo!' said Cate. She spread her arms. She had a quilt around her shoulders. She was holding a glass. 'Do you want some? It's Tasmanian whisky.'

'I'd better not,' said Franca. 'I don't like drinking when I've got to drive with the kids.'

She sat down. Sonja slid her a smile. She worked at the Koorie care facility in Bairnsdale. Once she'd told Franca, *Sometimes when I finish I need to be alone for a bit.* She had wild pale eyes. *I just know if I go home and the kids and Cate are hanging off me, I'll do something awful.*

Franca liked to think they understood each other.

'How's Clive?' Cate asked.

'Oh—not good today.'

'Have you heard of anyone else from Hazelwood with it?'

'No. He's lost touch with a lot of the blokes from work.'

'I imagine,' said Sonja, 'that'd be the sort of illness that men don't understand.'

'I was thinking. Remember all that talk about asbestos a couple of years back?' said Cate.

'You don't get chronic fatigue syndrome from asbestos,' said Franca.

'I know that. You just can't help wondering if somehow—if there's something—' said Cate.

'*Anyway*,' said Sonja. She began to rake her hair into a braid.

Franca watched her brown hands working away. 'It's not that we're really struggling,' she said. 'It's just that we've got no safety net. If the car needed a new windscreen tomorrow, we'd be buggered.'

The wind had picked up by the time they were heading home. On the radio there was talk of storms and flash flooding.

'Know what Cate told us today?' Emily asked.

'Hm?'

'"You can't bullshit a bullshitter."'

'No,' said Franca. She craned her neck to check if it was safe to pass the car in front. 'That's true.'

'Mum, Emily said *shit*.'

'It was in direct speech,' Franca said, batting at the indicator. She could feel Kurt's foot through the back of her seat.

'She said it twice. She said "You can't—"'

Gold headlights streaming towards them, the dull blare of a truck horn. One of the kids shrieked. Franca jerked the wheel, overcorrected. The car behind honked its horn, too. Someone was crying.

'Will you two *shut up*?' she said. 'We're fine. Nothing happened except this *fuckhead* in front is travelling thirty kilometres under the limit and I'm trying to get home.'

Her arms were weak with shock. She could barely hold the steering wheel. She wondered if this was how Clive felt all the time.

The house was unlit. The kids dropped their schoolbags at the front door. Franca heard the thud of their bodies against the beanbags, the fight for the television remote.

Clive and Billy were where she'd left them. There was a box of Duplo upended at the foot of the bed.

'Have you two been there all day?'

'We had some lunch,' Clive said. 'We played Lego. We watched some footy on YouTube,' he said, 'didn't we, mate?'

Billy smiled at Franca, then burrowed his blonde head into the pillow. He looked dopey, stunted.

'He needs sunlight, Clive.'

'I'm sorry. I had a bad day.'

'So he could have gone to childcare.'

'We don't have money for that more than once a week,' Clive said. 'You're the one keeps saying it.'

Franca knelt to gather the coloured blocks. They made a hollow clatter.

Clive's face appeared above her. 'Sorry, babe,' he said.

'I'm going to Mum and Dad's for tea,' she said, 'remember?'

'Oh, yeah.'

'I said you didn't have to come if you're not up to it.'

He touched her hair. 'What if I stay here with Kurt and Em. I'll make us dinner. You just go with Billy.'

Her parents managed a motel in Omeo. This time of year it was filled with people on their way to and from Hotham, rich people who stopped overnight before they fitted their snow chains and drove up the mountain to ski.

Used to be that Clive always drove. Franca hated driving the Great Alpine Road at night. She still hated it—the 70 kilometres of high-beam light, the sudden twists, the narrow places—but she had no say in it anymore. Clive hadn't been up that way in months. She wished he could see it now. It looked healthier since the drought had ended.

Her mother cooked a roast. Franca was embarrassed, turning up with only Billy in her arms. There was too much food.

She tried to tell to her parents about the meeting. She thought if she could explain it, she might understand it better. She thought of the lawyer. *That's why the CPI forecasts are low; everyone knows that.*

She felt sick.

'This happens time and again,' her father said. 'Remember how worried Clive was about the carbon tax? Thought he'd lose his job? It all blew over.'

'He lost his job anyway,' Franca said.

'Well, not because of the tax. All I'm saying is, the agreement might still get voted down.'

'We could move closer,' her mother said, 'and look after Billy.'

'Don't be silly.'

The rain fell in sheets.

'I should move the car. I parked under the big tree,' Franca said.

'Do that. Then sleep here tonight,' her father said. 'No good going home now. It's bloody cyclonic out there.'

She stayed in one of the motel rooms. It smelled of eucalyptus cleaning product and old carpet. She undressed Billy and tucked him in. She turned on the television. The football was just finishing. At home, the kids would be watching the same match. Maybe Clive would have made it to the couch, too. The muscles in her thighs had begun to ache.

She waited all night with the baby in her arms but the sunrise didn't happen; the light just got grey. She stripped the bed so the cleaner wouldn't have to. She washed Billy's face and rubbed a flat cake of soap between his tiny hands. She sat at her parents' table. Her mother scrambled eggs in the microwave. On television they were reporting the storm damage.

'Lucky you stayed here,' her father said. 'They've had trees down all along the highway. Flooding from Traralgon to Paynesville.'

'They just had a bloke in Bairnsdale,' her mother said, 'reckons almost the whole town's without power. You spoken to Clive?'

Franca shook her head. 'His phone might be dead. If there's no power, he won't be able to charge it.'

There was a tree across the road at Doctors Flat. She stood in her parka, hopping from foot to foot, while the SES crew finished clearing it.

She stopped for petrol in Bruthen. She tried calling Clive again.

'Was your power out?' she asked the guy at the servo.

'Nah, we were fine, but they were rooted in Sale,' he said.

'You been listening to the radio?'

The roads were slick with water that hadn't drained; flooded in parts. Franca pictured the footy oval in town. It'd be marshy. Maybe Kurt's match would be called off. She hoped their spouting at home had withstood all the bark and leaf shit, but she was sure she'd be up there all afternoon with a pair of gloves and a garbage bag, clearing out the muck.

She saw it as soon as she pulled into the driveway. The great dead red gum had come down. It lay across the yard, the priestly trunk like a spear. The front room of the house was caved in; roof beams exposed, weatherboards splintered to matchwood.

The caravan, the kids' room, was cleaved in two. It looked absurd, the metal folded into itself.

Franca heaved open the car door. She saw a striped doona cover beneath a sheet of corrugated detritus. She saw her daughter's gumboot. She started to run. Suddenly she was on her knees in the mud, calling for Clive. He was in front of her. His mouth was moving. He helped her up.

'They're okay,' he said. He was shivering. Franca clutched at his arms. 'The kids are inside,' he said. 'They're okay.'

VOX CLAMANTIS

When Johnny told me his mother was dying, really dying, I didn't know at first what he meant.

'They said ten months first,' he said. 'Then they said three. Now they're speaking in weeks.'

Speaking in weeks. Like that was a language.

On the phone he sounded fine, just tired. I knew he was living in a new place but I pictured him standing in our old kitchen, kneading his forehead with his knuckles, the frontal sinuses where he got pain. I pictured him standing in the bathroom with its pond-green tiles, with that big window that opened out to a view of a vacant lot. He liked to stand there when he was on the phone.

'I know it's really weird,' he said. 'I would never—ever—want you to feel like you had to do it. I'll understand.'

He would have rehearsed that call.

I said I'd come. Speaking in weeks.

I packed some things. I phoned work. I met my friend Suze for coffee. She kept saying, *I don't believe it.* She really was appalled. She said, 'I want *you* to be mad about it.'

I shrugged. 'He's not forcing me to go.'

'So why would you?'

'He's not a bad person. It just seems like the right thing to do.'

'What the fuck, a *bad person.*'

He called again that evening. He asked how much money I'd be losing, not working. I told him not to be silly. He was insistent. I didn't know how to be graceful about it.

The bus from Tacoma to Portland took three and a half hours. It was the time of year for white skies. I couldn't see Mount St Helens at all. I'd offered to drive down, I'd said we could take my car. He said no. I wasn't going to argue with him. He came and met me at the station. It was midday. The Greyhound depot stank of piss and other people's cigarette smoke. He was waiting. He put his hands on my arms. He kissed my hair. The first thing I said was *I'm sorry.*

We went to Blueplate, I think more out of custom than nostalgia. Afterwards he drove me back to his new place. It was in Mt Scott. We stood in the kitchen.

He rubbed his eyes. 'Listen, I'm sorry, but I have to work tonight.'

'It's okay,' I said. 'But what are they going to do without you for the next couple weeks?'

'It's not my problem once I'm out of there, but it is until I go.' He opened the refrigerator and stood looking in at its contents. 'There's consommé in there if you want it. I'm just gonna throw it out otherwise. Um. There's bread.'

'It's okay,' I said again. He nodded.

I didn't trust his new place, on the other side of the city. I made up my own bed on his fold-out sofa. He hadn't said when he'd be home. I locked his front door and started up Woodstock, towards the university. I'd lived in this exact neighbourhood when I first moved to the city, when I'd gone to college for dance at Reed. After you've gone to college for dance there's not much you can do except low-budget music videos and Disneyland, so I did both of those things. I worked for a year in Anaheim, long days, first cartwheeling down the clean cartoon streets in the twice-daily parades. Then it was six months as a character actress. I was a princess look-alike. Tiana, from *The Princess and the Pea*. That was what I was doing when I met Johnny. He thought it was real funny. I hated the way he told his mother, the way he made it quaint. I think he even said, *Can you believe that's a job?* and Cathy frowned and said, *Of course it's a job, John, Christ. There are all different important ways of earning a living. Cab driving's a job, grave digging's a job, Jesus Christ, John. This is not how I raised you.* Discussions of class disturbed her in the way they could only disturb the west coast bourgeois.

She always told people he was a *chef*, not a *cook*. She said his name more when she was frustrated with him.

When the Disney contract expired I was finished with it all. It's a short-term prospect. The Australian girl and the Portuguese girl I'd worked with said they were done, too, and went home. Over dinner Johnny's mother said, *Maybe you need to go to New York.*

We moved to Portland and I went to school for nursing. It felt good to be back in the cold with all those trees. At OHSU our scrubs were pine green. Johnny and I had lived in Goose Hollow. For a long time it felt like a new sweet place we'd carved out for ourselves. I never wanted to tear a hole in it until later.

• • •

In the morning he was up and about, showered before I'd dragged myself off the couch. It wasn't even light. I wondered if he'd slept at all. I pulled the blanket up over my face and watched his figure moving around the kitchen through the wool. At last I heard him carting bags out to the car. It was my cue to get up. There were two travel mugs of coffee ready to go on the bench. Johnny came back inside, saw me standing with my ass to the heater.

'I kind of wanted to hit the road early,' he said. 'You know, it's just such a long way, and—I'm sorry.'

'No, no, of course,' I said. 'I can get ready quick.'

That first day was mostly strange. We didn't speak until we were out of the city. I watched it get light through the windscreen. We'd barely talked about his mother. All I knew was this:

1. She was dying.
2. She wouldn't say it, but she wanted to see Johnny settled before she went.

Johnny's mother was what my mother called, a little disparagingly, a *bohemienne*. But she wasn't; it was just that she'd always had the money to do more or less whatever she'd wanted. Cathy had come from a Palos Verdes family, she'd studied at Berkeley, then she'd taught Comparative Literature there. She was a small woman. She moved like a dancer. She wore classic navy trousers with the cuffs expertly turned.

Palos Verdes family, Frank Lloyd Wright, Toluca Lake meant nothing to me before Johnny. When I met him I'd never seen the ocean.

He didn't show it to me.

We'd been separated for almost five months. I'd been in Tacoma for four.

Speaking in months.

Still, though. I couldn't believe he hadn't mentioned it to her. Somewhere near Eugene I said, 'I sort of can't believe you never told her we split up.'

I guess that surprised him, as a first thing to say.

'She loves you, Abby,' he said.

'She doesn't love me. She loves the idea of you being married.'

I guess he agreed with that.

'They could make a reality show about us,' he said at last.

'Two exes forced to behave civilly on a three-day road trip.'

'I feel like my dying mother is a very crucial part of this,' he said. 'Anyway, we're civil, aren't we?'

We don't speak enough to know, I thought, but I just said, 'I guess we are, Johnno. I guess we are.'

We made good time. After Grants Pass he headed out west, and we stopped in Brookings for gas. I got out to stretch my legs while he filled the car. We stood either side of it.

'How come the coast?' I asked.

'This is shitty enough,' he said, 'that I want to do anything I can to make it less so. And anyway, if I ever have to drive the 5 again, I'll kill myself.'

It was windy and our voices were straining over the car.

'It's going to take longer,' I said.

'A couple hours,' he said.

I thought maybe an extra day, but I didn't say it. If it were my mom, I wouldn't be driving at all; I'd be in an airplane and there by afternoon, but you can't pass judgement on other people's grief. Maybe he needed time to warm up to it.

We went to a bakery for coffee. It was right on the highway, in a strip of shops. I knew the ocean must have been beyond there, but I couldn't see it. While I waited for Johnny to piss, I smoked

151

a cigarette standing in the parking lot. I looked out at the lumber-yards. The smoke made ashy columns in the sky.

When he came out he said, 'You started smoking again.'

'Yes.'

'I'm sorry. I feel like that's probably my fault.'

'Not everything is about you,' I said. He laughed.

Things were easier after we crossed state line. He played Loudon Wainwright.

'Where are you working these days?' he asked.

'At a blood bank.'

'Huh,' he said. He considered it. 'You don't ever get bored?'

'I mean, no more than you got bored of flipping fancy burgers at Fred Upstairs,' I said. 'It was the first thing I got. Anyway, I don't have to be there forever.'

'I guess you don't,' he said.

It was strange not knowing each other.

'Does your sister know we've split up?'

'Of course she does,' he said. He looked offended. 'It's just Mom. You know.'

'I just want to be sure,' I said, 'who we're pretending for.'

We drove another five hours, and by the time he got to Ukiah, he was tired, and we decided to stop. I was feeling guilty I couldn't drive his stick-shift, even though I'd offered to bring my car so I could share the work. Once he'd tried to teach me to drive his old car, but it didn't work. We'd finished up yelling at each other in a field somewhere near Astoria.

We passed a Super 8. It said VACANCY in neon letters. Johnny slowed. He said, 'Wanna give it a try?'

'Super 8s,' I said, 'are where people go to fuck.'

'And we are absolutely *not fucking.*' He said it shrilly, in mimicry of someone I didn't know, or couldn't recognise, and I started to laugh. At the next exit we found a place. I left him in the car while I went in. I came back with the keys, we parked the car, we stood at the threshold of the room as I fumbled with the door handle.

I went in first. I took the bed furthest from the door, threw down my bag. I flopped on the mattress with my arms stretched over my head.

Johnny stood with his duffel bag slung over his shoulder.

'Separate beds,' he said. I tried to work out his tone. I rolled over onto my stomach. The room smelled like Pine-Sol.

'We are absolutely not fucking. You said it.'

I realised then, too late, that he was sad, and I was sorry I'd been flippant. He sat down on his bed, on his side of the room.

Before we went to sleep we both fussed around some, pantomiming bedtime like children in a toothpaste commercial. I laid out my clothes for the next day at the foot of my bed. Johnny phoned his sister. I felt like I should leave the room. I showered and changed into my pyjamas. By the time I opened the bathroom door again, let all the steam rush into the cold motel room with its twin queen beds, he wasn't on the phone any more.

'How is she?' I asked. I was towelling my hair.

'She is not good,' he said slowly, 'and I don't think Nina is great, either.'

'You could fly. Sacramento or SFO. You could be there in the morning.'

'What would happen to the car?' he asked.

'Just park it. You can come back for it.'

I moved to the bed where he sat, on top of the duvet. I took his face in my hands. I pressed it to my belly. I stroked his hair.

153

'We're partway there now,' he said.

I lay on my own bed again and tried to read, but I was tired, and my eyes kept moving over the same lines. One time I put down my book and looked across the room. He was staring back at me, propped up on an elbow.

'Why did you come?' he asked.

'I would always come,' I said.

When I was a kid, my sister and I had shared a room for years. Our beds were like these ones, parallel, pressed against the wall on either side. The floor between was where we played and fought. Then came the consciousness of space, and at some point we'd drawn an imaginary line down the centre of the room. Each of us would become enraged if the other encroached on her side. A gym sock, a tap shoe, a library book. On the other hand, if one of us left something desirable in that grey area—a pack of scented erasers, a candy bar in the pocket of a jacket—it was quickly claimed by the other sister. This Ukiah motel room, hundreds of miles away, suddenly reminded me so much of that childhood room, that cold demarcation of space, that for a second I had to think about where I truly was.

When I righted myself, I sat up and turned off the light. The switch was on the brick wall, at the midpoint between our beds.

I was almost asleep when he said it:

'You're the only person I could have asked.'

I thought my heart would break.

In the morning he sat inside the car while I finished my cigarette, standing in the glare of the headlights, and when I took too long he blasted the horn. It was a ridiculous, big-dick horn. The sky was still pitch dark.

'People are sleeping,' I hissed at him through his open window.

I stubbed out the cigarette and walked around to the passenger side. I slammed the door as I climbed in.

'No, why don't you shut it a little louder,' he said. 'I don't think the whole town quite heard that.'

'If you're so worried about time you could have taken the fucking 5.'

We argued about which way to go. 'If we go through San Francisco,' I said, 'we will get stuck for hours.' He said we'd miss the peak-hour traffic. He said, *How many times have you ever driven this route.* I said, *How many times have you.*

We didn't even look at each other for hours. He stopped in some tiny town for coffee. On the wall inside was a sign, one of those ones with the white letters that you can rearrange yourself. It said:

CARTER'S RESTAURANT
THE LORD OUR
GOD IS MERCIFUL
AND FORGIVING
EVEN THOUGH WE
HAVE REBELLED
AGAINST HIM
DANIEL 9:9

I asked for my coffee to go and walked dozens of circles around the parking lot outside. I looked in, once, and Johnny was holding the phone to his ear, passing his other hand through the steam rising from his cup. Back in the car I said, *Was that your sister,* and he said, *No.* I knew he was lying because he sniffed, touched his wrist to his nose.

When we were gridlocked on the Richmond–San Rafael Bridge I looked straight through the windscreen.

'Johnny?'

He took a real long time to answer. 'What.'

'Eat me the fuck out.'

I was so mad I fell asleep, like an infant. When I woke up we were out of the city again and I was sorry for being petty. He was allowed to be mean. His mother was dying.

In Monterey we heard the seals barking before we were out of the car. The wind was gritty; the sun poured out of the sky as if through a gash. I remembered staying with him here one summer. The motel had been right by Cannery Row, with enormous pictures of Steinbeck on the stucco walls. We'd both started to read the novel. Neither of us had finished it.

He parked by the water. Ukiah, Brookings, Portland, Tacoma all seemed a very long time ago. He said, 'Can we just be nice for a couple of hours? Can we please just be pleasant about this?' I nodded. I felt ashamed in a dull way. I touched the back of my hand to his. We hooked our smallest fingers together like kids making a promise.

We walked out on the pier. The air smelled fishy and cold. I bought us each a sandwich, fresh salmon and Philly on white bread, and we both said we were surprised at how hungry we were. The gulls made a sound like falling sheaves of paper when they took off all at once.

We climbed the stairs at the end of the pier. There was a row of small dinghies tied neatly down below, painted in blues and whites. I could see dirty rainwater sliding over their wooden decks.

'What are we going to tell your mom?' I asked.

'I think...I mean, just nothing. She thinks we're still engaged. We don't need to tell her anything particular.'

Our sandwiches had come in a paper bag, and he was folding

and refolding it, running his thumbnail over the creases. 'What did you tell your mom?' he asked.

'Just what happened. Just that it ended.'

'Did you go home?'

'No. I just said we'd wait for Christmas.' The sun was in my eyes.

'Did you tell her it was my fault?'

'I didn't. But she would think that. Mothers always take their children's side.'

He nodded then, and I nodded to the boats. We began the walk back to the car.

Only about an hour later, his sister phoned. We were on a winding stretch so closed in by redwoods that Johnny had thrown on the headlights.

'Hello, Nina,' he said. 'Hold on. I need to put you on speaker. I'm driving.' He fiddled around with his cell. He glanced at me. 'Okay. I'm in the car. With Abby.'

'Hi, Abby,' his sister said.

'Hi, Neen. I'm so sorry to hear about your mom.'

'Thank you,' she said. 'Johnny. Are you there? How much longer?'

'We're just about at Big Sur,' he said. 'I guess we'll be another five or six hours. I guess it depends on the traffic coming in.'

'What the fuck are you doing out there?'

'We took the 1.'

'You did, huh. You took the fucking 1.'

'We'll be there in a couple hours.'

'I don't know what will happen in a couple hours, John.'

Speaking in hours. Her voice sounded just like his.

We were out of the forest. The sky was wide and bright again. The ocean right there, where it had been all along.

'I can't get there any faster now,' he said.

'I needed you to be here faster two weeks ago,' she said. 'This isn't some fucking cute road trip. I don't know what will happen in a couple hours.' She'd reached a crescendo. She breathed. She said, 'I apologise, Abby.'

She'd disconnected before either of us had a chance to respond. Johnny yanked the phone from his dash. He held it in front of his mouth.

'NINA—YOU—ARE—A—CUNT!' he screamed, with a kind of intensity that must have made his guts tremble. 'FUCKING—CUNT!'

'Johnny.' It seemed the whole car was shaking with his fury. The air shimmered with it. I prised the phone from his white fingers. 'Pull the car over. Stop driving.' He must have been doing eighty miles. 'John. Stop the car. I'm scared.'

He pulled the car over to the shoulder. It skidded some, lurched there by the redwoods. He threw open the car door. He crossed the highway. I got out uncertainly. I shut his door and stood there dumbly. I was frightened to follow him. I had a feeling he was going to do something crazy.

All he did was yell.

When I say all he did.

It was the saddest sound I ever heard in my life. There were no words, just him with the pain in his lungs, bellowing out smoke from the grief in there. It seemed to me as if all the world, the redwoods and the cliffs and the ocean and whatever birds were out there, was recoiling from him. Johnny was screaming at the ocean, and I was crying but I hadn't realised it, and my mouth felt slack, like in those dreams where you want to speak but can't, and then Johnny was hoarse. He took a last lungful of air, spat it out with his broken voice. He crouched on his haunches in the grass.

I crossed the road. I knelt beside him.

'I'm sorry. I'm sorry,' he said.

'It's okay. I'm so sorry for you. I wish there was something I could do.'

He stood unsteadily. 'We have to go.'

'I don't want you driving,' I said.

'You can't drive a stick-shift,' he said, and flung out a hand towards the car. He sounded deranged. He had mad eyes.

'Then you can fucking teach me. I don't want you driving.'

We stood by the roadside.

'We can't stay here,' he said.

'I hate how you've—*rigged* this so I can't escape. I can't drive that stupid car.'

'I hate how you're acting like I plotted this. You didn't have to come.'

'Of course I did,' I said, amazed. 'Of course I did, you fuck.'

I was so on edge I thought I might kill him. I said, 'What about that motel we stayed at last Christmas?'

'She's at Cedars-Sinai. We're only five hours away. I really just want to get there. Abby.'

I thought of him last night in the dark, saying, *You're the only person I could have asked.* I thought of him last time we'd been here, standing on a boulder hundreds of feet above the edge of the Pacific Ocean, saying, *I like things that make me feel small.*

'I don't want to get in the car with you driving,' I said again.

'I'll be safe.'

We were both destroyed. We got back into the car. I wound down the window for that cold, clean air. Brine and soil and spruces. The sky was mother-of-pearl, the ocean was silver. The engine turned over. Johnny accelerated gently, to show me he was keeping his word.

• • •

It was almost 8 p.m. when we got to the hospital. Nina came to meet us in the cafeteria. I was moving like a puppet. I kept having to remind myself that she hadn't heard her brother calling her a fucking cunt and screaming at the ocean. She'd calmed down, too.

'I appreciate you coming,' she said to me. I shook my head. I was sitting beside Johnny, and both of us opposite her, at one of the cafeteria tables. She looked exhausted. She looked just like Johnny. 'She was conscious today, you know, lucid. It was the first time in a few days. I told her you were coming.'

'Thank you,' said Johnny. 'How is she now?'

'I mean, she's asleep again. But the nurses think she can hear. You can go on over.'

He stood. I did, too.

'I'll come with you,' I said.

He touched my arm. 'Maybe tomorrow,' he said. 'If she's tired now. You know. I won't stay long. I think I just want to be alone with her a second.'

Nina walked him over to the Becker building, then she came back to sit with me. We were mostly too tired to talk. I didn't want to drink any more coffee. I kept looking at her face, smooth and weary, under the fluorescent lights. She'd smile at me. She kept saying *Thanks for coming all this way with him*, as though the distance were the weird part of it all.

In the morning he went straight back to the hospital. I brought in our things from the car. Last night we'd arrived and collapsed in our clothes. I went from room to room and pushed open the windows. The air was light and fusty. Something in me wanted it to be nice for Johnny when he got home. I wiped down the surfaces that had begun to collect dust, I tipped water on the houseplants. I threw out the milk, the newspapers, the blackened avocados in the fruit bowl. I stood in the kitchen until my breathing matched the puffing of the net curtain at the window over the sink.

He was gone all day. He didn't say much when he got home. It was already getting dark.

'Nina is with her now,' he said. 'With the kids. I told them to come, since she was awake. Neen keeps saying she can't believe it.'

'Have you eaten?' I asked.

He shook his head. 'I thought I'd come home now while the others are there. If you don't mind—I thought maybe after dinner—I thought maybe we could go back.'

'Of course,' I said. I would have done most anything he'd asked.

The front yard was pretty in the cooling hour. We walked the six blocks or so, sat in a window to eat our burritos and watch the rain.

'She was worse than I thought,' he said.

'Did she know who you were?'

'Yeah.' He wiped his hands on his jeans. He stacked the plastic yellow baskets one inside the other. 'Nina said she rallied. Said she'd hung on for me.' He laughed like he didn't believe it.

'It happens,' I said.

'She's working tomorrow.'

'I'll come with you then, too.'

We walked back to the house, got into the car, headed straight there. I hadn't realised I was nervous about seeing Cathy, but when we pulled into the parking lot my palms were damp and my heart was going fast. I was sad for the first time.

'She's not hooked up to anything anymore,' he said as we waited for the elevator. 'I didn't know that would happen.'

'Yeah, that's how it works,' I said. 'I guess it is kind of shocking.'

'It seems barbaric.'

'It's the best way,' I said.

The door to her room was open. Before I saw her bed, I saw a rubber mattress on the floor, where I guess Johnny had spent the day, and Nina before him. Nina's kids were sitting there now, quieter than I'd ever seen them. The boy had his fingers in his mouth. I thought about how kids and animals know things. And then I saw her, crabbed and shrunken in her white sheets. The last time I'd seen her, she'd been the kind of woman you'd describe as 'petite'; 'diminutive', even. In that bed in the Becker building, there was something foetal about her. She was asleep. Her mouth gaped open like a baby bird's. I saw her heart thumping beneath her pyjama shirt—midnight blue, silk, with cream piping around the collar and cuffs. It seemed like it might tear through her chest.

Johnny and Nina nodded at each other. The kids barely registered our arrival, but I bent down and whispered *Hi*, and the boy crawled into my arms. I felt his toddler weight fall against me.

Johnny sat on the edge of the bed. He touched Cathy's forehead, like a parent checking for fever. 'Mom,' he said. 'Mom. I'm back. I brought Abby. Abby's here.' He had to try a few times, but eventually her lids opened and her fingers twitched. I saw the fury of her body trying to pull itself into the world.

'Yes,' she said, like he was telling her a joke. She smiled. Her eyes closed and opened. 'My loves,' she said. I moved to kiss her forehead. Her skin was dry.

'Hello, Cathy,' I said. I slipped my hand in hers. I think she squeezed my fingers, but I could have imagined it.

'Oh, I'm so happy you're here,' she mumbled. 'There's not enough hours in a day. Or we're greedy. I'm not sure which.' She tried for a laugh. Her chest was heaving in an obscene way. Nina and Johnny were looking at each other with something I registered as wonder, shaking their heads, wide-eyed. I realised this was the best, the most alive, they'd seen their mother. Nina whispered, *She hasn't spoken since the weekend.*

'You look beautiful, Cathy,' I said.

'I just wish I got to see more of all of you,' she said. 'Yes. He's always so busy, isn't he, Johnny. What do you suppose he does all day?' I almost laughed. Her eyelids flickered. Her heart thumped away obstinately.

Outside the room Johnny said, quietly, 'She's so thirsty. This is barbaric.'

'It's how it works, Johnno,' I said. 'I'm sorry it's like this. But you have to know—this happens all the time. I know it's hard to see, but I promise this is all normal.'

Nina emerged from the room. She had the baby on her hip. Her daughter, the older kid, hung in the doorway.

'Thank you for coming,' Nina said. 'That was incredible. I'm glad she saw you both.'

'She would have wanted in-home care,' Johnny said in a low voice.

Nina nodded. 'Well, thank you for being here when I had to make that decision. Thank you very fucking much for making yourself available.' She looked down at her children, as though she were surprised to find them there.

Johnny and I didn't speak until we were in the parking lot. Then he said, *Thank you.* He said, *You are a very good little actress.*

We got home and began to fuck like it was nothing at all.

Our bodies were confused. It was like coming home.

'I miss this,' he said.

'You don't. You don't.'

'You don't know.'

'Stop saying that.'

163

We were in the guest room. We were lying on its bedspread, duck-egg blue. I wasn't certain I could fall asleep beside him, but every other room seemed a strange choice.

'Do you think we could have ever made it work?' he asked.

I sat up. I fished around for my sweatshirt. 'No, Johnny.'

'I know,' he said. 'I love you like I love myself.'

'You hate yourself.'

'I don't *hate* myself. Sometimes I just kind of—can't bear it. You know what I mean?'

'No.'

'God, Abby, you're being a real cunt. You're being so hard.'

'I'm a cunt,' I said. 'Your sister is a cunt.'

'Well, don't talk to me like I'm a stranger.'

'I don't know how to play this,' I said helplessly. 'You can tell your mom whatever you want but we're acting. That was a past life.'

His face scrunched up in an ugly way. He was crying.

I got up and closed all the windows. I ran a shower. When I went back to the guest room he'd fallen asleep on top of the covers. I went to his sister's room, and dragged her duvet to the couch.

In the morning I heard him talking to the woman next door. I looked out the window at him. He was wearing a sweatshirt that must have belonged to Nina once. Dartmouth, its crest, white on pine green, the motto: VOX CLAMANTIS IN DESERTO.

We drove back to the hospital. The traffic made me hostile. I said, 'I hate this city.'

'You wouldn't if you'd grown up here.'

We were on the freeway. I was feeling like I'd rather get out and walk.

'I hate Wichita,' I said. 'I grew up there.'

'Wichita is the butthole of the earth.'

'Don't talk about it like that.'

'See,' he said. 'You don't hate Wichita. Anyway, there are nice parts of LA.'

'Like what.'

'The dog park up on Mulholland.'

'The dog park.' I started to laugh and couldn't stop. I didn't care if he'd been serious or not. He was laughing, too, both of us weak and sobbing with it, there, not halfway to the hospital. We just *could not stop.*

Cathy passed away before noon. Johnny was with her. I was downstairs on the street, walking around in the sun, on the phone to my own mom. As soon as I set foot back in the room, I knew what had happened. Johnny was sitting on the rubber mattress on the floor, his legs spilling onto the linoleum.

Nina was already on her way in. It didn't seem fair that she hadn't been there, with all the vigils she'd kept. She arrived with her husband. She touched Cathy's hands, folded; then her cheek, then her hair. She looked from Johnny's face to mine.

'You can stop now,' she said.

But we sat there for a few hours more. None of us was in any hurry. Cathy looked younger than she had in years. All the pain had gone from her face. She was newborn.

In the family house that night I fixed us a lazy supper. We watched the evening news. There had been a mudslide in Washington. Two boys were still missing. Their father hoped they might be alive; trapped, somehow, in a pocket of air in the mud. After we ate Johnny went down to the cellar and came back with a bottle of Bryant Family Cabernet. He said, 'I'm an orphan now. We might as well.'

We sat out in the yard to drink, on the heavy lawn furniture. I smoked and he did, too. The phone kept ringing inside. After the fourth call he disconnected it. I was very tired. The garden was cool and closed in with pines and oleanders and other things I didn't know the names of.

He slept in his childhood room and I went to the guest room. In the carpeted hall that led from one to the other, we stood opposite each other, and he kissed me with his devastated, expensive wine mouth. He held my face in his hands. He said: 'You were great.'

HUNGRY FOR GOD

This was the part of the memory she didn't tell anyone: him stand-ing in the drive, ready to burn. The silence after she cut the engine. The country darkness was a heavy clean black, the stars sharp, but he was washed in light from the porch and her car. When she got closer she saw he was trembling, shivering, crying; wild hair and eyes, jerry can in his hands.

They were young then. Twenty, twenty-one.

He did burn down a house eventually, and that was where their friendship ended; there, or after the terrible six months they spent living together in the apartment in Griffith; or when he dropped out of school and disappeared; or when he came back and took to her car with a tyre iron—but all that came later. This was when they were new, still learning each other's ciphers.

• • •

They were both scholarship students and they liked to joke about it sometimes. She was the only brown girl in their residential college, he was the only poor kid. July, after exams, they left Canberra for the holidays. Nisha to the Melbourne suburbs where her family lived, Callan to his mother's house in Jerilderie. They sent letters. This was 1993. She wrote him eight pages about her cousin's wedding, a drily funny account of the day, each new paragraph neatly indented. The legal pad paper was thin, like the pages of a bible. Her looping script darkened when he held it up to the window. He wrote to her once the first week—*It's sort of maddening now that I'm here*—and twice the second. He phoned one evening in the third week. Her mother answered.

'It's one of your university friends,' she told Nisha, her palm over the receiver.

Nisha had few friends in Canberra. Still, she was surprised when it was his voice.

'It's really bad,' he said. She heard him breaking.

She told her parents the truth: her friend was sick and she needed to go help him. He lived in the country. His home was not an easy one.

'You can't leave *now*,' her father said, but she did. They could see she was worried. They didn't fight her. She threw books and bags and shoes hurriedly into the boot of her old Corolla, and her father re-packed it all into tidy mountains. He tucked twenty dollars for petrol into her hand. Her mother gave her food in plastic containers, a thermos of tea. It was only when she was an hour up the Hume that she felt a spasm of sorrow at leaving them.

She did not stop except to call him once from a servo payphone, scribbling his directions on the inside of her wrist. She hadn't thought about what would happen when she arrived.

The night was so black, the road to his house unmade. She drove slowly and still stones rained against the car. The house dawned on her suddenly, and him, too: he was barefoot, wearing only a singlet and boxer briefs. He was thin-limbed, streaked with dirt, shivering. The jerry can trembled in his arms.

She got out of the car. The fog moved in the headlights.

'It's okay,' she said. She kept her distance, as if from a feral animal. 'I'm going to take you back to college. I need you to put down the petrol.'

He nodded, and dropped the jerry can at his feet. He looked relieved, like he'd only been waiting for her permission not to set the world on fire. There was snot on his face.

'Is anyone in the house?'

'No.'

'Okay. We're going to go inside, pack your stuff, and go. All right?'

He nodded. Her fingers buzzed with the memory of the steering wheel. The road was still vibrating in her bones.

In his childhood bedroom she helped him pack clothes and books into an Ansett duffel bag. She folded his T-shirts like a mother, like a housekeeper, only permitting herself to look around when he left the room. It was cold and spare. A peeling poster of the solar system on the wall. Cheap desk in pale pine; grime and scuff marks on the skirting board; plastic venetian blinds blown out. His height from age eight was marked on the doorway. She watched him grow in increments to her eye level, then taller.

He threw his toothbrush and razor into the bag, yanked at the zip.

'Ready?' she said.

He lurched at her. She almost reeled backwards before she

realised he was reaching for her. She touched his hair, his neck. She smelled petrol and sweat.

She drove for hours. He slept beside her like a man anaesthetised. A boy. His face turned young when the vigilance left it. Later, this was how she liked to remember him. And yet: so much of his beauty was the mania that crackled around him like static. He was never more alive than at 3 a.m., the morning of the exam, pacing around her room as he recited the required knowledge of reflexes and homeostatic control; or performing a hot-shoe shuffle in the common room, kebab in hand, after a night out; or jogging beside her in the grey, frigid mornings, arguing about entropy. The damp Canberra cold got into her lungs and burned her sinuses, but he was never out of breath.

She let herself feel pleased, in a narrow way, that he'd trusted her enough to call. She wanted to keep him. Not in the sense of possession—just to contain him somehow, somewhere safe. Her car shuddered in the wake of the road trains that passed in the other direction, lights ablaze.

Once she stopped to piss by the side of the highway. She was squatted and shivering, one palm to the hood of the car for the warmth, when she heard a keening. She knew it was a fox, but it sounded just like a baby. She pulled up her jeans in a hurry.

He was still asleep, slack-mouthed, when she pulled into a roadhouse not far from the city. Neon steam rose from a neon coffee cup hanging in the window. A sign above the petrol prices promised HOT CHIPS AND CAPUCCINOS. She felt dazed. She went around to the passenger side and opened the door. He did not stir.

'Wake up,' she said. 'Callan. We're going to get breakfast.'

'Breakfast?' he said.

'How long since you've eaten?'

'Hm?'

'I said—'

She took off her glasses and rubbed her eyes. His head fell against her. She felt the warmth and weight of it on her sternum. She cradled him. She touched his lank hair, stroked his cheek.

'Come on,' she said.

He followed her across the car park, dutiful as an old dog. She'd never met someone less interested in food. He ate only when he remembered to, and because his body demanded it. He'd once told her that growing up, his mother had made tomato soup by diluting tomato sauce in a cup of boiling water.

They sat by a window. Their own faces shone back at them. It was still dark out. There was a sliver of silver-blue at the horizon. The floor was crunchy underfoot; the table smeared with dishcloth streaks. Nisha scraped her hair into a stumpy ponytail and watched him squint at the laminated menu. He still hadn't decided when the waitress came back for the second time. Nisha ordered him coffee and an omelette.

'You were sleeping like the dead,' she said.

'Sorry.'

'Don't be. You must have needed it.'

He put a hand across his eyes. 'I haven't slept in nine days,' he said.

She nodded. 'I'm going to the bathroom,' she said.

She washed her hands and face, scrubbed the biro from her wrist. She felt jetlagged. She looked at her watch. It was not even twelve hours since he'd phoned. For a brief moment she imagined her body, another one, still reading on the floral couch at her parents' house in Mulgrave. Her father would be getting up to go to work soon. *What are you doing on the couch? Turn on the light. You'll strain your eyes.*

She sat opposite him again.

'Did you notice anything? When you went to the bathroom?' he asked.

'What? Have I got something in my teeth?'

'No, no, no, no, no. Look at my face. Can you hear anything?'

His voice was conspiratorial. One knee jiggled up and down beneath the table. Nisha felt unease rising in her.

He leaned over the tabletop and gripped her chin so she couldn't turn her head. Their faces were very close.

'It's not a trick,' he said. 'What do you hear?'

'Just normal kitchen noises,' she said at last. 'I don't know. Highway sounds. People's conversations.'

'*Huh!*' he said triumphantly. He released her jaw. She looked around gingerly. It dawned on her as he spoke.

'There is not another table here,' he said, very quietly, 'with more than one person sitting at it. Every single person in this place is talking to themselves.'

The waitress brought their food. They ate in silence, struggling to hold in laughter. They tried to tune in to the frequency of the chatter around them, but the words overlapped and hummed and tripped. It was hard to make out whole sentences. Once, though, the man at the table closest to them put his head in his hands and cried *Oh, I am* hungry *for God!* with such ardour and desolation that the scene stopped being funny. Callan trowelled forkfuls of oily yellow egg into his mouth until his plate was clean, then laid his head on his arms. He looked up at her and gave a sleepy smile. She could picture him as a baby.

'You look all right now,' she said.

'There are craters in the moon we need telescopes to see, bud,' he said in an American man's voice, and if he was quoting a film she didn't know it, but she smiled at the table.

She pulled her toast into strips.

'Let's get out of here,' she said at last.

Canberra was blue at dawn. The college was empty. His room looked unlived in, though he'd been there only a few weeks ago. Nisha thought of his childhood bedroom. What evidence there was of him on this earth was very little.

He dropped his duffel bag on the floor. 'Will you stay?' he asked.

'I'm just down the hall,' she said. He lay on the single bed in his clothes and blinked at her.

She fell back on the couch across from him.

'Get a blanket,' he said.

'I'm okay.'

She planned to leave once he was asleep, but she dropped off, too. When she woke it was after two in the afternoon and her neck was stiff. Her hand grazed the cinderblock wall. The room was fusty with their unshowered bodies, unbrushed teeth. She rolled over and looked up through the window. The sky was bloodshot with blossoms.

Later he'd tell the story; they both would, and in the same way, although they had not seen each other in more than twenty years. They both redacted the beginning and end. The roadhouse restaurant full of loonies was the difficult punchline. There was no reason offered for the night spent driving from Jerilderie to Canberra; it was just a long-ago thing that happened at university. Each of them shed their name to become *a friend*, clean and vacant and anonymous.

Callan remembered other things about her that never fit into the retelling. Her child-sized hands. Her spasms of laughter, which were so rare, so unexpected, that they tore through him like a forest fire, too. A few years later, in medical school, they'd learned to suture on pig trotters. Hers were spectacularly neat. Everything was so easy for her. She had two cassette tapes in her car when she came to get him—Baby Animals and L7. She wore ratty flannel shirts that slid off her shoulders. The terrible time, when they were twenty-three, when he'd betrayed her in front of her parents— longing, suddenly, to hurt her and her kind, tight-knit family—and it started the argument that ended their friendship.

He remembered himself at that time, too, so full of hunger. Too ravenous to ever sleep. The books he'd read, at first to keep up, then to tread water, then to know things for his own pleasure. How happy he'd been! He wanted to have long hair so he could wear it the way girls did in winter, tucked into the collars of their jumpers and coats.

He saw her on television once. Just a flash, a fragment. It was in the years when he had a night job cleaning aeroplanes. Walking through the empty terminals, he saw the same news clips play over and over from wall-mounted televisions. And there she was, older but unmistakable. *Children are remarkably resilient*, she'd said, and some other things. She was talking about a toddler who had survived a horrific house fire. Her name and position at the Royal Children's Hospital floated on a banner beneath her face, but he recognised her before that. Was it strange they'd wound up living in the same city? Perhaps not. Her face still filled him with a fearful love. The terminal was as silent as a mausoleum. He stood beneath the screen.

PRESSURE OKAY

He heard that the MTC was putting on *Summer of the Seventeenth Doll*. He remembered studying it, and he remembered Kirsten studying it thirty years later. He phoned her and asked if she'd like to go. Or it could have been her idea. Maybe she'd sent him one of her text messages. A photo of the advertisement on the side of a tram and a stream of question marks, like one of those puzzles in the paper where you had to make meaning from two oblique images. He didn't remember precisely what the play was about. Something about men attracted to strong light, the way the sugarcane grew straight, yearly pilgrimages. He bought the tickets, anyhow.

His daughter worked at the university. She was interested in everything to do with women being included, or not included, in revolutions, from the French one through to the Arab Spring. She taught classes on subjects Wes couldn't altogether believe existed. On occasion he'd gone to visit her, or meet her for lunch. Even though he recognised her office as meagre, he was frightened of the sandstone it lurked within. The sight of the academics moving across the courtyards with their blue lanyards; the students with their friends and mobile phones and impossibly young faces; the cordoned-off smoking areas all made his guts heave. He felt sure someone would recognise him as an impostor and drag him out at once, away from this place where his daughter was so at ease, and back to the funeral home where he worked. She knew the names of the staff serving coffee from what seemed, to Wes, to be a shipping container planted on one of the pale brick paths.

The train was late. He waited on the platform. He watched a car speed away from the city down Station Street. Its headlights shone on the train cables overhead. The light moved along the wire like an animated image of neural propagation he'd once seen. It was raining. He could smell the sea. When the train arrived, water glittered on the windows.

On the seat beside him was one of those free street papers, folded in two. He read it idly. There were mistakes in the copy that he, with his Form 5 Blackburn Tech eyes, could pick. It gave him a small, mean satisfaction. The horoscope section was titled *Should I get out of bed tomorrow?*

He shut the paper.

He watched two boys standing on the metal platform between the carriages so they could smoke their tailored cigarettes. The taller one stepped back inside the train, smoothed his hair like a young James Dean. There was an angry salvo of pimples along his shaved jawline. His eyes flicked over Wes and down the train.

Wes felt small. He wanted to be worth a fight.

• • •

Kirsten was waiting for him outside the theatre. She was wearing a dress that looked like a shirt and a black coat she'd had for years. As he got closer, she was finishing off a plait in her hair. She smiled at him. She did an absurd wave with her elbow as her hands worked away. It seemed impossible that he and Miranda could have produced this creature, blonde with hard, flat cheekbones. Viking daughter, early bloomer. When she was only eleven or twelve she'd had wide hips and long limbs and Miranda had said *She'll grow into it all.*

'Have you been waiting long?' he asked. She shook her head. She touched her cheek to his.

He had been to the theatre before, but not for years. He'd forgotten how you had to go down into the earth. The thick carpet, the gold light, the brass rails, like a spiffy crypt.

They propped against a wall to watch the other patrons.

'There were these kids on the train,' Wes began. *I don't want to get old*, he thought, and *I am very lonely.* Kirsten was looking at his face as if she expected the start of a story; something funny or awful. He touched his hand to his back pocket. 'I'll get us a drink before we go in, eh? Do you want a glass of champers?'

'Whatever you're having,' she said. He lurched to his feet.

When he returned she'd found a sofa. They clinked their glasses together.

'Kir,' he said, 'have you ever been to one of those places where you walk in and they do you a massage on the spot?'

'Your neck still giving you trouble?'

'There's this new massage place near the Woolies,' he said. 'One of those walk-in joints. A leaflet came in the post.'

'If your neck is sore,' she said, 'you could go to the chiro.'

Wes grimaced. 'Don't they crack you?'

'Yes, but it feels wonderful. The whole purpose is *realignment.*'

He must have looked unconvinced. 'I don't know, I was sceptical but I started going for my back. Then I stopped getting tension headaches, too. Anyway,' she went on, 'there's something sort of meditative about having someone just work on your body in silence for half an hour. You feel very relaxed.'

'Half an hour,' Wes said. She looked at him. They both recovered.

The play was different from what he remembered. He was shocked at how it turned in his guts, at the end, when Roo—or was it Barney?—was on his hands and knees, pounding his fist at Olive's feet. He wanted to say something to Kirsten about it, as they emerged into the foyer with its gentle light, but he heard an older woman say, *I certainly think she was miscast for the role*, and he lost his nerve.

They went for a nightcap. They both ordered boilermakers. Wes did not drink often anymore, but when he did it was most always with Kirsten.

'What have you got on tomorrow?' he asked when she returned with their drinks.

'Just jobs,' she said. 'I've got to do really boring stuff. Weed the garden. Mark some essays, clean the bathroom. Tomorrow night I'm going to Tom's parents' for tea.'

Tom was a good bloke. He worked in the courts, a juvenile liaison officer or something along those lines. He barracked for the Tigers. The first time they'd met, Tom had cooked dinner at Kirsten's house, pasta with pippis he'd collected himself. He was Kirsten's first boyfriend in two years, which meant her first boyfriend since Miranda had died. First Christmas since, first trip to Bermagui since, first birthday since, first parking ticket since, first flu season since. Wes had thought they were all over and done with, and then Tom came on the scene.

Wes liked him, but he wanted to know what Miranda thought.

He said goodbye to Kirsten at the taxi rank. She folded herself into the back seat and waved at him from the window as the cab pulled away. He walked back to the station. His veins were warm and all the stars were out. He did not drink often any more, and when he did it made his head swim. Going home he watched the Richmond skyline flatten out as the train clattered away to the suburbs. A girl, a child, vomited onto the floor at the far end of the carriage. Her boyfriend covered it with one of the free street papers.

Wes put his head to the cold perspex and tried not to smell the vomit.

From Tom's parents' house, she sent him a photo from her mobile phone. It was a picture of her with their whippet. It looked up at Kirsten lovingly, ears cocked forward. Kirsten's face was impassive, even sceptical. They'd never had dogs when she was growing up, because Miranda had an allergy.

It was a funny picture. Almost immediately after the image was transmitted came the caption: *THE MALE GAZE*. She'd done it to get a rise out of him, to make him laugh. He sent a text message back: *Har har.*

Wes didn't mind feminists so much. He believed in equal pay, he just didn't know why they needed to be so shrill about everything. Sometimes it seemed to him as if Kirsten saw everything as an attack. He didn't understand all the talk about *emancipation*.

Years ago he'd said to Miranda, *I thought it was something she'd get out of her system while she was a teenager.* His wife had looked at him and laughed. She'd said, *That* is *the system.* Maybe he'd answered with something thick, because he remembered Miranda looking at him with something like pity or patience and saying, *Darling, that's the only way for women to survive.*

He hadn't thought about it in years. Remembering it now made him ache in a new, hot way; that his wife and daughter had shared it, that he couldn't access it, that it wasn't his to understand. He was sitting on the couch watching a Sunday night program on skyscrapers being constructed too hastily in Shanghai. He'd eaten pork chops for dinner. The plate was on the coffee table. Every so often he ran his finger around the rim, where salt and apple sauce had congealed. He kept his phone on the table, where he'd see it if it lit up or vibrated, but Kirsten did not send another message. It was probably good, he thought. It'd be rude to be tapping away at her phone in front of Tom and his parents.

He waited a few days, and then called her when he got home from work.

'Are you free for dinner on Sunday? Bring Tom. I'll do us a roast.'

The sliver of silence meant she was surprised, but she recovered.

'We're supposed to be going to a lunch down the peninsula,' she said. 'It's my friend Naila's birthday. At a winery down there. But we could swing past on the way back. We'll just have to pace ourselves at lunch.'

'All right. You just tell me what time suits you. It might be a step down from the winery, though.'

'It'll be lovely,' she said. 'How was your day?'

'We've got a new kid. I had to take him for his first transfer today.'

Wes worked as an undertaker. It was a serious job, and it suited him well. He liked the quiet spaces and the ceremony and the driving. When Kirsten was four or five, she'd gone through a phase of being fascinated with death. Miranda had said most kids did. For months, she'd interrogated Wes not just about his job, but about all sorts of things. *Will there be a light in my coffin?* she'd asked. *I need one for my books.* She'd told her kindergarten teacher she wanted to be an undertaker. The teacher, who only knew that Miranda was a nurse, was horrified. They still laughed about it.

'Was it an old people's home?' Kirsten asked.

'Hm?'

'The transfer.'

'No, it was at the Alfred, actually. This kid's only been on the job for ten days. He's nineteen. I was worried about respect,' Wes said. 'You know. I half-expected him to say, *What does it matter, he's dead,* but he was very respectful.'

'Kids aren't animals.'

'I know,' he said, 'but I was still waiting for it. It's hard to teach that sort of thing.'

'They're not animals, Dad,' she said again. 'Or—*we're* not animals. Whose side should I be on, anyway?'

It was cold enough that he didn't worry about leaving the groceries in the car.

When Miranda was alive, she'd always bought a cooked chook for a homeless bloke who sat outside the Woolworths when she did the grocery shopping. Kirsten had mentioned it once, and that was the first Wes had heard of it. *Where is he now?* Wes said. Kir looked helpless. *I don't—I don't know,* she'd stammered. *He might have moved on.* By then Miranda was gone and he couldn't ask her about it.

He locked the car again and walked back towards the lit strip of shops. He passed a travel agent, shut for the night. He looked in at the red-and-white poster advertising fares to Launceston,

Coolangatta, Sydney. His only thought of Sydney was with Miranda, when they'd been newly married. It was hot. She'd worn these ridiculous sandals with heels, and he'd just about had to carry her around the harbour. In the photos they stood in front of the Opera House with shy faces. They looked embarrassed to be standing in such pulchritude.

He passed the newsagency, an opportunity shop, a brightly lit shopfront selling frozen yoghurt. The employees inside looked pained. They were wiping down the immaculate stainless-steel benches in rhythmic circles. It looked like a strange modern dance. Who'd be eating frozen yoghurt at this time of year, thought Wes. Then the massage place.

It was empty. Bunches of fake flowers hung from the ceiling in lurid blues and purples, suspended by their plastic stalks. Wes stood at the desk. The room was deep and narrow. On one side was a row of four chairs, all facing the window. A bright green curtain had been hung across the glass. Wes remembered reading once that green was calming, easy on the eyes. Maybe someone had told him—it could have been Kirsten or Miranda. Below each chair was a small plastic basket—for keys and handbags and things, he supposed. On the other side was a series of curtains in that same green fabric. It reminded him of the emergency ward at the hospital. The one nearest to him was open. He could see a massage table covered with folded towels.

'Hullo,' he called uncertainly. He was embarrassed.

A young man appeared from the back of the shop.

'Good evening,' he said, beaming. 'What would you like?' He pushed a laminated price list across the counter at Wes. The grid swarmed before him: he reached for his eyeglasses, and couldn't find them. He pointed blindly at the page.

'I'm just after a neck and shoulder massage, please.'

'Of course. This way.'

He sat Wes down at one of the chairs. There was a series of posters on the wall above the window. One of them looked very old. It said REFLEXOLOGY in English at the top. Underneath was a foot sole, divided in cheerful colours and annotated in what he thought to be Chinese. Another poster showed a man's body from behind, colours and lines streaming from it.

'Sir, you can remove your glasses, if you want.'

For some reason he'd imagined a woman. The kid put a towel around Wes's neck, a small one, the size of a dishcloth. It was velvety. Wes looked at the green curtain in front of him, blocking out the view of the street, the car park. There was music playing. Piano and panpipes. He could hear two young women speaking in a clipped-sounding foreign language in another room, maybe a television, too. He could hear tyres on wet gravel outside. He closed his eyes.

The kid ran his thumbs along Wes's spine, the bit right at the top, beneath his skull. His fingers moved and made arcs below the shoulder blades.

'Pressure okay?' he asked.

'Yes, yes, it's fine.'

He'd imagined a woman. He'd imagined Miranda at his neck, her small, strong hands. She made him shiver.

The young man started high up. His thumbs pressed hard. They made circles. It seemed he was battling the muscle, or trying to get it to relinquish something with his stubborn hands. Once or twice Wes almost cried out at the strange pain. He felt his body tense. He knew the kid could feel it, but all he said was, *Okay, sir?* and Wes said, *Yes, it's very good.*

He thought of twilight sleep. He thought of Kirsten, aged five, standing on his back, walking up and down while he lay face-down on the floor. He thought of his wife in the surf at Bermagui, bobbing to the surface after being pounded by the ocean, the water dripping from her hair and nose. The hands went all over. Wes thought of the play the other night. There'd been a scene inside the house, but with fireworks out on the street. Somehow it had all been constructed so that the shadows and blaze of the pyrotechnics were suggested through an open window at the back of the set. He thought of his wife hanging from the monkey bars at the local playground, teaching Kirsten how to swing from rung to rung. He thought of rain sound machines. He thought of a place he and Miranda had once gone for lunch to celebrate something or other. It had been high summer. There'd been tall windows over green lawns, expansive gardens, hydrangeas. Miranda telling him about the flowers. Their colour changed according to the acidity of the soil. *You can bung a couple of nails in,* she'd said, *and get a crop of really blue ones.* Damp, heavy splendour.

The hands changed. Suddenly they were like hard, flat rain. Fingers pelting down his neck, his shoulders, his arms. Wes felt the skin there jumping under the kid's fingers, rapid-fire. He was waking up.

At last the young man clapped him on the shoulders.

'Okay?' he asked.

Wes cleared his throat, came to. He opened his eyes. The light was stunning. 'Thank you,' he said.

At the counter he opened his wallet and saw the flyer inside, advertising twenty-five per cent off. The special opening rate. With his specs on, he looked at the price list again. He saw that his massage had only cost twenty dollars. He didn't want to use the discount anymore.

He kept saying *thank you* while the young man handed him his change and receipt and loyalty card. He staggered out into the night. His car was in the Woolworths car park, where he'd left it, groceries in the back seat. The milk was still cold. He exhaled. His breath hung before him.

The tree in the backyard was heavy with lemons. Wes had a mind to make a cake with them. Miranda used to do something she called lemon bread. It was dense. She'd served it with clotted cream and berries. When he found the recipe, though, it called for separated eggs and glacé lemon, and he'd never done any of that. He sat down at his computer and found a recipe for a lemon pound cake instead. He found a converter to change all the American measurements to metric ones he could make sense of. He set all the ingredients out on the bench.

He was on his hands and knees beneath the lemon tree. He was singing to himself—*And did those feet in ancient times walk upon England's mountains green? And was the holy lamb of God on England's pleasant pastures seen?*—when he saw a flash of colour at the back door. His daughter's boots, blue dress. She stood on the back porch with her arms crossed, looking down at him.

'Hullo.'

'Hullo, love.'

They were both embarrassed. He didn't know why he'd been singing a hymn.

'I know we're early,' she said. He saw Tom standing behind her. 'We were driving back from the peninsula. It seemed silly to go back to the city, then come all the way out again.'

'Well, it would've been silly. I'm glad you're here. You can help me grate these.'

He stood with his hands full of lemons. His knees were damp: the wet ground had soaked through his trousers. He kissed Kirsten's cheek. Shaking Tom's hand was an impossibility while he was still holding the fruit, so he grinned and said, *How's it going, mate*, and Tom said, *Good, mate, let me take some of those for you.*

Inside Kirsten handed him a bottle of shiraz. 'We brought you this from the winery.'

'It was what we had with lunch,' said Tom.

'You didn't have to do that,' said Wes. He turned the bottle over to examine its label, but he couldn't read anything without his glasses. He set it on the bench beside Kirsten's handbag.

'The chicken'll be another hour,' he said.

'Oh—take as long as you like. We had a huge lunch—' Kirsten said. She looked at Tom and laughed. Wes turned to check on the vegetables.

After they'd eaten Kirsten and Tom washed and dried the dishes standing side-by-side at the sink. Wes inspected his cake. It had cracked on top, but it smelled good.

'Mum would've just put icing sugar on it,' Kirsten murmured, looking over his shoulder. They did shy smiles at the cake.

'Oh, no,' Wes said. 'I forgot the bloody cream.'

'Doesn't matter,' Tom said. 'It smells amazing. We don't need cream.'

'Oh, no,' Wes said again. He was paralysed. 'Hang on—I'll run down to Woolies and get some. We've got to have cream.'

He felt in his pocket for his wallet. He saw Kirsten and Tom look at each other.

'I'll go,' said Tom. 'Just regular cream?'

'Regular. Thickened,' said Kirsten. She squeezed his fingers. The front door slapped open and shut.

Wes made them each a cup of tea while they waited.

'I went to that Chinese massage place.'

'Did you? How was it?'

'Terrific,' he said. 'My shoulders feel sort of—lighter?'

'Had you ever had one?'

'Not for years. Once your mother and I got massages in Bali.'

'Well, that was years ago.'

She was drawing the teabag up and down in her cup, releasing whatever was in there. Wes watched her. 'It was almost as if I didn't know how bad I felt,' he said, 'until I didn't feel like that anymore.'

'Once,' Kirsten said, 'Jules and Olivia gave me a voucher for a massage for my birthday. It was at one of those swish spa places. They did a facial and all this other stuff. Hot stones. Anyway it was a full body massage and it went for an hour. And before the woman started, she said, *Sometimes people experience very strong emotions during the massage, or just after it.* Something about the emotion being trapped in the tissue.'

'Tom's a good bloke,' he said.

'He is.'

'Are you in love with him?'

'I think Mum would have loved him more,' Kirsten said. She made a sound like a cough or a sob, but her face was laughing. 'I don't know if Tom and I—if this is all there is. Is this it?'

Wes heard the car pull up, the handbrake, outside in the driveway.

'Dad,' Kirsten said. She sounded frightened.

COARSEGOLD

|

In Coarsegold our life was slow and small. Lux was the one who'd suggested the move, but she was the one who went crazy with it. I took a job teaching at Mariposa County High. She worked as a receptionist in a motel in Oakhurst, seven or eight miles up. She dyed her hair the colour of sunshine sometime around then. I remember us in the bathroom of the new old house. Her hair was wrapped in plastic. She was sitting on the edge of the tub, one foot propped on the enamel and the other lifting the linoleum from the floor where it was coming unstuck. We were both smoking cigarettes, both in our underwear. The window was wide open. Those months were real hot. Too hot to smoke, we said, but kept at it anyway. I painted my toenails. The dusty grit from the bathroom got caught in the varnish. That was more or less how it was there.

It was summer when we moved in. My brother Jeff drove up from Fresno to help. The house hadn't been lived in for a long time. Everything was coated in a film of sticky dust. We painted the skirting boards, sugar-soaped the walls, hung a drugstore calendar in the kitchen.

In the front room two things had been left behind: a dirty mattress on the floor and a message on the ceiling, written in black marker—

THAT CRAZY FUCK HE DONE IT ONE TIME TO MANY HE LEVING IN A COFIN

Lux lay on the filthy mattress, tucked her arms behind her head.

'What do you think she meant,' she said. 'One time, but to many women? Or, he's pushed it too far, one time *too* many—'

'Gives me the willies,' said my brother. He stood in the doorway as if he weren't going any further. I pushed past him and began to take down the net curtain, blackened with grime.

'It's just a room. They don't live here anymore,' Lux said.

'Anyway,' said Jeff, 'how do you know it was a woman wrote that?'

'It was a woman,' Lux said.

She had no patience for my brother.

We painted over the message. We pulled up the carpet tacks. That room became our bedroom.

It was a hot summer, then it was a hot fall. Thursdays were Lux's night off. We went swimming in the Merced. I have this picture in my head of her, hair dripping wet, towel draped over her shoulders and tied under her chin like a superhero's cape; pale thighs, legs like two young shoots, hiking boots. We cooled off in the swimming hole. We only returned to the car when it began to get dark. We spread our towels on the seats (the car was still new enough that we cared about those things). In the parking lot by the Wawona stable, we kissed like a couple of kids. We were already hot again from the walk back. Her skin smelled of minerals, of the river. She wore this striped one-piece with a low back. She drove me wild.

We never ate dinner those blue nights. We'd stop someplace on the way home, one of the diners where the waitresses introduced themselves, for brownie à la mode or lemon meringue pie. I have this picture in my head of Lux, hair damp, American flag pinned to the wall behind her head; licking a spoon clean before she tried to balance it on the tip of her perfect nose. While she was at it my hand shot out and grabbed the maraschino cherry from her dish. She laughed and said, *God, you're such a fucking bitch, Joanna,* and we looked at each other's faces reflected in the window. Fluorescent humming above us. Love was small-town adventure, it was our knees touching beneath tabletops. It was Lux tearing open the saccharin sachet with her teeth and emptying its contents into her cup, then doing the same for me. The packets were pink. They said SWEET'N LOW. I always kept a few in my purse, just in case.

I'm saying this so you know: there was plenty of love. I don't know why I started what I did. There's no defending it.

His name was Perry. He was a junior, but he'd been held back a year. He was in my English class. He played football. His family was part of the sixteen per cent of the county that lived under the official poverty line. His daddy had a cabbage farm. His ma did something with the Department of Corrections, but he said she never worked these days, and I didn't ask more than that. We fucked under the bleachers. We fucked in his truck. We fucked in the pup tent in his daddy's backyard. We fucked in the dry creek bed in the summertime, and by the fall that secret place, that hollow in the ground, was full of leaf litter and muddy water. The earth bore no imprint of our bodies ever again. I was learning to think in a forensic way. I hung the sheets out to dry. I invented alibis. Lux never knew a thing. The truck-tyre marks in our drive could have told her everything she needed to know, but she was never observant in the way you'd expect. She could leave a pair of dirty pyjama shorts on the floor for a month and forget they were there, or a newly bought bag of fertiliser on top of the dryer. And anyway, she believed me good.

Lux was an addict when we met. I told her it was me or the smack. She laughed in my face, so close I felt the mean huff of her breath. She said she didn't respond to ultimatums. But she tried. Cold turkey, cold comfort. Cold sweats, she said, but I didn't see her when she was withdrawing that first time, so I wouldn't know. It lasted four months. When she relapsed she went to a clinic in Minnesota. That was where she'd finally gotten clean. The day she was discharged it was fifteen below freezing. I remember her in the snow. It was so early that the roads hadn't been salted yet. I remember her walking gingerly in the parking lot, laughing, dark rings under her eyes. 'What if I slipped now, broke my pelvis. They wouldn't be able to give me fucking anything.' We drove back into the cities, sat in a diner on Hennepin while she phoned her parents. She was crying, they were crying.

So you know—we'd survived things. Small fights, money stuff, new cities, lost jobs. Once she'd been 5150'd when we lived in LA.

They called me at work. I was at Centennial High then. There had been riot police there that very week on account of a student brawl, and that's what I pictured when I heard she'd been committed, but apparently it all happened very quietly. It was her therapist who made the call, nothing dramatic like you see on TV, and, when I went to visit, Lux wasn't raging or violent, just sedated out of her fucking mind.

I don't say this to absolve myself of anything: Lux could be hard work, but that wasn't why I started with Perry. Anyway, everybody is hard work in their own way.

Late in the fall it was too cold to go swimming, but we hiked the different Yosemite trails. My body felt strong; I was making new muscles. On the weekends we sometimes drove to Fresno or Merced, once to Death Valley. I took a picture of Lux standing at Dante's View. She pointed things out to me, recited their names. Funeral Mountains, Telescope Peak, Badwater Basin. We laughed when we looked at the photo properly, back in the car: all the majesty of the valleys and mountains, and she was standing, frowning at me a little, with a hand to her brow for the sun, like she was waiting for a bus. Coming home we hit bad traffic. The sky got dark while the car rolled and stopped.

'What the fuck is going on?' I said. I punched the steering wheel.

'We can't do anything. We'll get home eventually,' Lux said. She was good at waiting. At last I realised why we'd come to a halt: blue and red party lights outside. There had been an accident. Beside the road was a field and that's where the car had ended up, in two bits. There was something on the road; a bundled, ragged shape. I stared for a second. Lux reached across. She took my chin in her hand, hard, and forced it so I was looking out front again.

We didn't speak for almost a half-hour. Close to home I said, 'Did you see? There was something on the road.'

'It might have been an animal,' Lux said.

II

Lux worked evening shifts, which suited her. She was a poor sleeper and liked having the days to get things done. Without ever saying so, Perry and I created this plausible charade where he came by after school with his books, as if I were going to teach him something. He parked his truck out back so it couldn't be seen from the road. We didn't talk about any of this. We just had the same ideas about things. When I told him I was sorry, he knew what I meant. He didn't ask beyond it. On the last Wednesday in October we drove to the lake, the artificial one out by Raymond, and fucked in the car there. *Might as well make it nice*, he said. I started to laugh and couldn't stop. I was straddling him, my back to the water. I was swimming on his body.

Afterwards we walked around the lake. He took a flashlight out of his glove compartment and shone it on the ground in front of us. It was cold. He wasn't graceful enough to offer me his jacket. I didn't expect it. There had been a good sunset earlier. Neon California sky, the kind that doesn't photograph easy. I'd stood out on the porch to watch it. Now everything was grey and blue.

'You ever kill a snake?' Perry asked.

'I grew up in Minneapolis.'

'I had to do it this last summer,' he said. 'With a hoe. Had to cut off its head.'

'Make you feel like a man.'

'It kind of did,' he said.

'What are we doing,' I said. I felt ridiculous. We stopped walking. 'Take me home,' I said.

He turned eighteen.

'I'm having a party,' he said. 'Just at home. You want to come?'

His sense of humour was not so different from Lux's. I snorted. We were in my bed. His legs were heavy between mine. The room smelled of him.

'You want to see where I live?' he asked.

'What, you going to take me to meet your mom? I'm sure she'd love that.'

'No, dummy. I'll just drive you out there.'

It started with me humouring him, climbing out of bed and pulling on my shirt. I knew where he lived, more or less; he'd told me before, and I could have looked it up on his school records. But I realised he was serious, standing there with his keys in his hands. There was a nervous, tender part of him I only saw sometimes. When it flashed at me, it was like a warning signal.

We were quiet in the car. It was dusk, the time for animals to run out in front of the headlights. I watched the roadside for deer. He was playing a CD of awful heavy metal and at last I said, *This music is the worst*, and he grinned and turned it off.

'Tell me about your girlfriend,' he said.

'I don't want to talk to you about her.'

'Tell me something nice about her.'

'What the fuck,' I said. I looked at him sideways. 'What are you doing.'

'I just wanted to get to know you some.'

'I think you know me well enough.'

He was silent.

'I'm not your date,' I said, 'or your girlfriend.'

'I know. You're my teacher. And you could go to prison.'

'Yes. I could.'

We'd reached his house. The drive was long and unmade. There were no streetlights, but in the dark I could make out the metal husks of old cars and a tractor in the front yard; unmowed grass. He'd brought me here with purpose. He was showing me the house he'd grown up in, the house where he still lived with his mom. I knew not to underestimate him. A light flickered on at one end of the place, a small yellow rectangle of light. I tried to think of something nice to say, but I could barely distinguish the shape of the building.

'I'm not gonna tell anyone,' he said at last. 'You don't have to worry about that.'

Saturday was clear, unseasonably warm. Lux and I hiked the Cathedral Lakes trail. By the time we got to Upper Lake the sun was so high and hot that we stripped off and went swimming.

Lux ploughed right into the water, shrieking when it hit her ribs. 'It's cold!' she said breathlessly.

'It's November.' I was standing at the lake's edge, arms crossed over my chest.

She pulled a face and disappeared underwater. I saw a stream of tiny bubbles, then nothing. I had the sudden, foolish impression she was gone. The woods were silent. I crouched, naked. My nails dug in to the flesh of my arms. A forest of pine needles sprouted between my toes. I had to hold my breath to keep myself from calling her name. I counted to ten, then twenty.

She burst from the water, laughing, gasping for air. Her face was slick and dripping. She opened her eyes, saw me squatted there. 'What are you doing? Come in.'

I swam right into her arms. She hugged me from behind, both

of us facing the mountains. She kissed my neck, my temple. Her hand ran the length of my body underwater, traced a line right down my belly.

'You looked like a feudal woman giving birth in a field,' she said. We fooled around in the water. There was almost no way anyone would hike down here this time of year, but we still messed with each other. *Hello, sir. Nice day for it*, Lux hollered to a phantom man on the shore once while I was floating on my back. I flailed around in a panic. She cackled even as I pushed her under.

On the hike back our clothes stuck to our bodies. We were mostly quiet.

Lux walked in front. I saw the muscles working in the backs of her legs.

'Let's play a game where we tell each other something new. Something we don't know about each other,' she said over her shoulder.

'We know each other pretty well.'

'There's so much stuff,' she said. We were going uphill. I could hear the effort in her voice. 'I'll go first. When I was younger I was really self-conscious about my ears. That they stuck out.'

I almost laughed. 'Your ears are so normal.'

'I didn't think so. They were all I could see when I looked at my face. I thought I looked like a monkey.'

'How old were you?'

'Fourteen, fifteen, sixteen. I used to sit out in my dad's car in the drive, tape my ears back and scream.'

I was glad I hadn't laughed. I waited for her to say more, but that was the end. I tried to think of something innocuous. I felt my lungs fill with panic.

'Um. When we were kids, Jeff and I were messing around after school with some other kids from the neighbourhood. This was when we were living in Winona. Coming home we found this dog that had been hit by a car. It was still alive, but not by much. It was making this terrible noise.' I shifted my backpack. 'Jeff told me to wait with it while he went home to get our dad's shotgun. We were absolutely not supposed to touch it. I'm not even sure how he knew where the key to the cupboard was—Dad always kept it locked. I never saw him pick up the gun. We just knew where it was kept.'

'What happened?'

'Nothing. Jeff came back with the shotgun. He made me stand away and close my eyes, and he put it to sleep.'

'Put it to sleep,' Lux echoed. 'Is that it?'

'You didn't say it had to be a secret.'

'It doesn't.'

She stopped, heaved her pack off her shoulders, and found her water bottle. She took a drink, handed it to me. She started to braid her hair.

'Remember when we were first together, and we went to Seattle for a weekend, and we stayed with that friend of yours from college? Mike, or Matt, or someone?'

'Matt.'

'Right. I was still using.' She finished her braid. 'I stole $250 from him.'

'You what?'

'He left it right there on the table one morning. You know, he didn't strike me as the type to miss it, exactly.'

'He never mentioned it to me,' I said.

'Of course he didn't. How embarrassing for him. If he even noticed it was gone.'

'Matt wasn't loaded. That was a shitty apartment,' I said. It sounded weak.

Lux shot me a glance. She picked up her pack, shrugged into it and started walking again. 'Do you think we're too close?' she asked.

'What do you mean?'

'I don't know. I was just thinking. Maybe I depend on you too much.'

I was calcified with terror. I had to work very hard to put one foot in front of the other. I wished I could see her face. 'Why would you—why were you thinking about that?' I asked.

'I don't know. I feel like you're not always here.'

'I'm here. It's just us. You wanted to get out of the city. I thought you wanted this.'

'I do. It's not like that.'

'What's it like?'

She didn't answer.

By the time we got home she was late for work. She tore around the house in a sudden fury. I packed her some leftovers to take. I told her to drive safely. She frightened me when she moved that recklessly. She was like a hurricane.

The house was airless without her. I ate my dinner in front of the television. I wished we had a dog. I grabbed my keys and drove to Oakhurst, to call in on Lux, but by the time I reached China Creek I pictured her face—surprised, ready to laugh at me—and I was suddenly scared of what I might say to her. I made a left at the Golden Chain Highway, the way I drove to work every morning, only I went straight through Mariposa, too. I headed out to Midpines, where Perry lived.

It didn't feel crazy until I was at the bottom of his drive, idling by the parked trucks. I'd never thought of him as popular, but it seemed like the whole school had come to his birthday party.

The house was all lit up, and there was a bonfire in the yard. I could feel the vibrations of the music where I sat in my car. A couple of kids tumbled from the doorway, arm in arm. They were laughing or sobbing; I couldn't hear which. They started down the drive towards me. I wondered what would happen if they got close enough to see my face. I wondered if they were Mariposa kids, and if they'd recognise my car. By the time I'd played out all the scenarios in my head I was halfway home.

III

I fought with the head of department over the books. I took it out on Lux and the house, slamming the cutlery drawer, setting all our things rattling in the refrigerator, making dinner.

'It's the dumbest shit I've ever heard,' I said. Lux took the jar of spaghetti sauce from my hands, emptied it into the saucepan. She was wearing a black singlet. I could see the vertebrae of her neck. She spoke to the stovetop.

'You think you're maybe patronising them? I mean, you're talking like they're idiot hicks. It's Gatsby, it's not, you know, *Hamlet*. I'm sure they can deal.'

I fell back against the bench. I was irate. I started on about retention rates, their mock SAT scores, the kids smoking dope in the parking lot between classes.

'It's just dope, Joanna.' She gave a little laugh. She glanced up at me. 'I'm sorry. I just think it's funny.'

'What is funny?'

'You're so invested in them,' she said. She'd moved to the sink to rinse the empty jar. 'Like, you're having this *Dead Poets Society* moment. It's this saviour complex of yours.'

'What the fuck is that supposed to mean?'

'Oh, fucking *nothing*, all right? I'm sorry I ever said anything, Jesus—' and then the jar hit the cupboard above my head and the glass splintered. Three big pieces, and some smaller ones too many to count. It looked worse than it was but we both shook and she held my face in her hands and said, *I'm sorry I'm sorry I'm sorry*, and kissed the cut, she kissed the glass, there was blood on her lips and in my eyelashes. I sat down on the floor. My peripheral vision was starry. I hung my head between my knees. I said, 'You know what, Lux, *you* fucking come and teach those kids. Come and teach them.'

She said nothing. She drove me to the ER with one hand on the wheel and the other pressing a cold compress to my forehead, saying nothing the whole time.

It was too late for the clinic so we had to go all the way to Madera. I told the nurse I'd tripped on the stairs holding a glass. Lux stood with her arms crossed and her lips pressed together. When we got back into the car she pulled her shirtsleeves down over her hands and looked out at the hospital.

'Sorry,' she said. 'I'm sorry, baby.'

'It's fine. You saw. It was only a couple stitches.'

She shook her head. 'I can't believe I did that.'

'Hey. It's okay. I came home salty. I was in a foul mood.'

'What if it had been worse? I'm sorry.'

'Please stop saying that,' I said.

'I'm scared of myself,' she said. She was pressing her hands together between her thighs. Her arms were shaking. I touched her hair.

'Why don't you let me drive home,' I said. She shook her head again. All I could think was that I was letting a teenage boy fuck me from behind, and she was the one who was feeling bad.

At home the spaghetti sauce was cold on the stove. It seemed funny now. Neither of us wanted it anymore. Lux threw the entire thing into the trash can, saucepan and all. I couldn't stop laughing. I told her it didn't hurt.

'Maybe we should buy some plastic tumblers in case I freak out again,' she said. She looked so destroyed that I started to kiss her mouth, her neck. The glass was still in pieces. There was blood streaked, dried brown on the linoleum. I said, *We can worry about that tomorrow.* We went to the bedroom and loved each other very hard.

In the morning Lux redressed the cut like an expert. I said, *Thank you, nurse* and we fucked again and I was late to work. In the parking lot I parted my hair on the wrong side to cover the bruise. I put on some lipstick. It was a cheap drugstore brand I'd bought without testing, and when I saw my face in the rear-view mirror my mouth was pale and cadaverous. I dug around for a tissue to wipe it off. Perry tapped on my window.

'Jesus.'

'Nope, only me,' he said. He grinned.

'I don't think it's good for you to stand here,' I said.

'I'm not coming to your class today.'

'Okay.' I got out of the car, slung my bags over my shoulder, shut the door.

'Can I come over after school?' he asked.

I looked at him. 'Do what you like.'

'What happened to your face?' he asked. I thought he was going to reach out and touch me. I flinched. He hadn't moved. The bell rang. It was like an air-raid siren.

'I tripped on the porch,' I said. 'I've got to go. I don't want to be up here with you right now. Come by after five if you're going to.'

We walked our separate ways across the parking lot, him towards the running track and me towards the faculty room. The straps of my satchel cut into my shoulder.

There was a scuffle down the end of the hall, teeming with kids. I could hear the sharp cuts of the boys' voices. *Why you gotta be so up in my ass about this?* I craned to see what was going on. A pair of hands to the chest. *I'll break your fucking neck.* I'd never understood their berserk violence, their energy for threats. My last school had been the same.

'Hey,' I called, 'it's too early for anyone to do any neck-breaking, okay? Get to first period.' A few heads turned, a few *yes ma'ams*. But the bodies kept swarming. They were directionless, circling. Someone fell against me, hard. I stumbled sideways into a row of lockers. Immediately a space cleared around me. Everything went quiet. A blonde kid, the one who'd knocked me into the lockers, held up his hands in a don't-shoot gesture.

'Sorry, ma'am,' he said.

'That's okay, Ty. It was an accident, right?'

'Right.'

'Okay, so don't worry about it. Get to class.'

I went to the bathroom and locked myself in a cubicle. I was shaking worse than last night. The cut on my head throbbed. I'd known the kids were just messing around. I never thought anyone was going to get hurt. There'd never been any threat. Still my blood was rushing.

In the faculty room I put on a fresh pot of coffee and checked my phone while I waited. Lux had already called to ask how I was.

Perry kept his word. He wasn't in my English class.

But that night he came round the back wearing his Grizzlies sweat-shirt and jeans, a half-hour after Lux had gone to work. He left his sneakers by the door. We fucked first in bed, my face pressed to the pillows. He said, *I'm close,* when he was about to come. I took him out of me and rolled away to the edge of the bed. He lay gasping like a fish on a beach. It had been a week. We fucked again in the bath, slower that time. I thought about saying, *I want to swim in your blood, I want to swim inside you,* but it would have been wasted on him, and, anyway, it wasn't true.

We lay in the tepid bath, skin gone soft under that milky water.

'I seen you and your girlfriend down at the Dirty Donkey last weekend.'

'That's got to be the worst name for a place, doesn't it?' I said. 'I don't remember seeing you there, anyway.'

He grinned. 'I wasn't there for long. It's kind of funny seeing your teacher knocking back two-dollar PBR and shooting pool.'

'Lux got off work early,' I said.

'Y'all could get married,' he said. 'It's legal here now.'

'I know it.'

'My mom told me. She thinks it's a good thing.'

'Does she now.' I couldn't keep from grinning.

'What? What's so funny? I just meant, if you wanted to, you could—'

'Perry, it's okay.' He smiled from under his hair. I settled against him.

'It's funny when you call me Perry,' he said.

'It's funny when you call me ma'am,' I said. 'Anyway, I'm not going to call you Tonto.'

He touched the freckles on my shoulders with damp fingers.

'Everybody calls me Tonto. My mom calls me Tonto. Can't be racist if she does it.'

I twisted round to kiss his neck. I tasted sweat, and it made me think that this was all hard work. I looked at our knees, mine smooth and pink between his, bony mountains covered in fine black hair.

'How do you know how to do it?' he asked.

'Do what?'

'You know, do it with me when you're…'

He wanted to be a man, but he was as curious and open and dumb as a child.

'Listen,' I said, 'I had boyfriends before.'

I'd seen photos of him from only a year ago, in the halls at school, in the old yearbook. He'd been younger even then. All lashes and boy bones, a crew cut I don't know why, I'd had no cause to ever ask him. He had a football player's body these days.

I sat with him while he laced his sneakers on the back porch.

'You doing anything on the weekend?'

'Just working for my dad.' He straightened, blinked. 'Smoke a bowl with the guys.'

We both laughed. He backed away and climbed into his truck. He flicked on the lights, horror movie high-beams. I lifted a hand to my face for the glare.

I always imagined we'd get caught but it never happened.

He wrote me notes on his composition pages in very light pencil so that I could erase all trace of him. *Meet me at the cornfield, meet me at the parking lot, meet me at the hardware store, meet me at the creek, meet me at the bleachers.*

Blue twilight at the running track. He made as if to leave when he saw me approach. He slipped under the bleachers.

The ground was grey and brown. It was foolish and risky to meet there. Everything we did was foolish and risky. I ought to have been paranoid about his wearing a condom, but it only happened about half the time. We never took any care.

I crouched down with one hand on the cold metal. 'I'm not doing this,' I said.

'It's done, ma'am.' He smiled like a man in the electric chair. The crepe streamers flapped damply behind his shoulders. He kissed me so differently from Lux. I never knew if I liked it or had just gotten used to it, habituated, acclimatised, whatever, his fast boy mouth. It was a funny position to be kissing in, crouched over the ground clinging to each other. I lost my balance. We laughed. Mud under my fingernails. I was a long time in the faculty restrooms, scrubbing it away. Once I'd asked him what he meant to do after high school. He said, *Work on my daddy's farm. Maybe move to the desert, get a job in a casino.* I think he saw me looking at him sadly, because he also said, *It ain't so bad, ma'am.* He was half-right. It only wasn't so good as to force him to make something of himself.

IV

It was December when Lux started talking about moving again. She brought it up when we were out at dinner. The paper wrapper around my disposable chopsticks had the symbol for double happiness on it. For a moment I thought, *She knows.* She knows and she wants to make me say it. It turned out she was just edgy for reasons she couldn't say. Maybe it was the cold, I said. It never got this cold in LA. Diurnal mood something or other, seasonal affective disorder. She went quiet, but started up again as soon as we got home.

'I've been thinking about it for a while, Jo.'

I knew she hadn't. 'I feel like we have a life here,' I said.

'You have a life. I'm sitting behind a desk reading Thomas Hardy novels with that goddamn door that tinkles every time someone walks through it. Handing out extra towels and maps.'

206

'I thought that's what you wanted. I thought you wanted time to write. Slow life.'

'I made a *mistake*. I got it wrong.' She fumbled in her handbag for her cigarettes. The pack was empty. She hurled it at the wall. 'I can't *stand* this place.'

We said we'd talk about it when we got back from New York. We went up there for the holidays, to stay with her parents. We saw Patti Smith perform at Webster Hall the night before New Year's Eve. Lou Reed had died not long before. She opened with a cover of 'Heroin'. Lux wept next to me. The intensity of it made me feel almost sick; the pulse like that stuff rolling and stopping in your veins, or how I imagined it. The steady, unbroken bass, the rising grief, the rapturous silent audience: a great, terrible build-up of pressure. At the final chorus Patti picked up the music stand she'd been using for the lyrics and moved it aside and started to dance. The crowd began to cheer and stamp and move in a new, joyful way. I sneaked a look at Lux. Her cheeks were a mess of tears and snot. Her body was moving with the throbbing horror of the music. She was weeping openly.

Her parents lived upstate so we'd booked a hotel room for the night. It was a Comfort Inn all the way out in Red Hook but we both agreed we'd been lucky to get anything so close to New Year's. We lay facing each other, each propped up on an elbow.

'How about that Lou Reed cover,' she said. 'I just stood there bawling.'

'I saw. I didn't want to touch you—you know, interrupt you. You looked like you were vibin' it by yourself.'

'*Vibin' it*,' she repeated. She looked down at the bedspread, touched it with her fingers as if reading braille.

'What were you thinking?' I asked.

'It was the only time I felt good in my skin,' she said. 'I had to give that up.'

I couldn't participate in those memories. She was making me sad.

Once she'd overdosed and died. She said she'd had a vision: millions of women shaking out their bedsheets to hang in the cold wind. She'd never made sense of it but she liked to joke. At the end there's no white light, just women folding laundry. She liked to laugh at herself when it was on her terms. It was the game she played with her junk days: it was everything but it was nothing. Whichever way I tried to understand her was wrong.

The day we left there was a snowstorm and our flight was diverted. I waited on the carpeted airport floor with our bags while she went to get us coffee. I watched her standing in the queue until her figure was swallowed up. She was wearing a placid expression, resigned to waiting.

I thought of my mother saying to us kids, *I've already given up so much of myself,* and how I might never say that to Lux because it would ruin her. Leaving her parents' house, we'd all stood at the bottom of the stairs to hug and say a long farewell. Her dad asked me, *Is she looking after herself?* I said, *Yes. Yes, everything is wonderful.* I knew he hadn't meant smack, but he added, *She doesn't like herself.* Who does, I thought. It had never been easy for any of us, in orbit around her.

I imagined telling her about Perry. I imagined the conversation we'd have. She'd stand with her arms crossed, tongue moving over her teeth. Or she'd say, *What happened?* And I'd say, *I became invisible,* and that would make her cry.

But back home things were fine. We drove too fast down the

highway from Sacramento and she sang along to 'Deanna', only she changed it to *Oh, Joanna*. Years ago, when we were first together, we drove to Idaho for a wedding. I remembered her asleep in the back seat on top of her suitcase. I drove all night. I told myself stories to keep awake. Maybe for a thing to be a good a long time, it has to be miraculous.

I didn't see Perry until the second week of January, when classes started again. I was feeling clear-headed. I gave my juniors a pop quiz, knowing Shannon Kendrick would be the only one to have made the chapter summaries I'd set before the holidays. I asked Perry to stay behind after class. I didn't want to have to do it, I said, but I was going to need to speak to a parent if he kept flunking out on everything.

'Ma'am, that was a pop quiz. That was a bitch act.'

'Don't speak to me like that,' I said.

He hung his head and smiled. His figure loomed over my desk. I picked up the paper with its red marks and handed it to him.

'That's it,' I said, 'I got nothing else to say about it. You can go.'

'Will I come around tonight?' he asked.

My eyes darted to the classroom door before I could help it.

He grinned again. I could have killed him.

'After five,' I said. 'You're gonna be late, you don't leave this instant.'

But Lux wasn't going to work. She was sick with a head cold. I filled the tub for her. I felt like I had a fever, too. It was already dark out. I broke the rule I'd never made. I called Perry. I said, 'You can't come tonight.'

'You're lucky,' he said. 'You just caught me.'

'I'm sorry.'

'I'm sure it isn't your fault.'

We hung there, speechless. I could hear Lux singing to herself in a clear, tuneless voice.

'You want to meet someplace?' Perry asked.

'I can't.'

'Okay.'

'Ten minutes,' I said. 'Meet me at the parking lot near the Round House. You know the one?'

'I know the one.'

I went to the bathroom. 'I'm just going to pick up some groceries. You want anything?'

'I thought you were going to stay here with me,' Lux said. 'I thought it would be nice to do something together.'

'You hate taking baths together.'

I sat on the edge of the tub. Her shoulders were freckled and pink with heat. Strands of hair stuck to her damp neck. I loosened her topknot, combed the hair between my fingers. I made a loose plait of it. The sunshine colour was growing out; the hair at her crown was the same colour as her brows.

'I'm five thousand per cent done with this,' she said, but she closed her eyes. She tilted her head to mine and began to kiss me.

'I'm only going to the store,' I said.

'Okay.' She drew her knees to her chest. 'I'm sorry. I'm so on edge. I don't know what's happening. I'm *crawling*.'

'It's all right.' I kissed her forehead. I picked up my keys. I put on my coat. My heartbeat was like Kalashnikov fire.

He'd arrived first. He was sitting with his lights off. I crossed the lot, slid into the suicide seat.

'I can't stay here,' I said.

'I never asked you to.'

The grey digits on his dash were blinking. I'd already been too long. I'd have to invent a shopping list, some reason I'd had to go to the next town. I started to unbutton my shirt, quickly; I reached over and fumbled with his belt, drew his dick out of his jeans, fit him into me. I wanted to be bored with it all but I wasn't.

At home Lux was out of the bath. She sat on the fold-out sofa watching TV while I put the groceries away, the ones we didn't need. I tossed her a packet of Tylenol. She'd taken her hair out of the plait.

'Are we getting like Jerry and Elaine?' she asked.

'I don't think so.' I threw up my hands, stuck out my neck, squinted a little. 'What's the deal with airplane food?'

She didn't laugh. 'You had to leave because you couldn't be in the same room as me,' she said.

'You're being ridiculous. I went to the *store*.'

'You know what I mean,' she said. 'Ever since we moved here I feel like I'm annoying you. I feel like you're outgrowing me.'

'I'm not outgrowing you. But I can't keep having this conversation over and over again. When have I *not* been on your side? When have we not done exactly what you needed?'

'Yeah, you're a goddamn saint, Joanna. There never was a woman as good as you.' She dropped her head. 'I'm sorry,' she said.

'I don't know what more you want me to say.'

'I wanted to move here because I thought it'd be easier to have it...just us. I wanted us to make a cocoon here. And it still feels like there's so much space. And you wouldn't understand that.'

'No,' I said, 'I don't.'

I sat beside her. Her hands were in her lap, palms-up, as if she were ready to receive communion. There was a pretty bruise on her forearm.

'I worship you,' I said.

'Who are you. You're speaking like me.'

'I want to swim in your blood.' It felt good to say it out loud, since I'd been rolling the words around in my skull for months. She looked at me like I was crazy. Her hooded sweatshirt was unzipped and slipping from her shoulders. She was flushed. I kissed her mouth. I kissed the hollows of her collarbone. 'What's the matter with you,' she kept saying, but her face was turned up to the ceiling. I thought about how we fit together but sometimes things were hard work. I thought about how giving up was giving in. I slid my hands under her pyjama shorts. She was warm. I thought about how, when we fucked these days, it was like a stream of tiny confessions. The springs of the old fold-out sofa were begging us and still we were moving over each other in a fever dream, now me supine and her above me, her thighs framing my face, her taste in my mouth. I thought about Perry, the way we fucked in our machine-gun, 7/8 time signature.

'I want it to always be like this,' she said. We knew how to love each other the right way. I thought, *Nothing is worth this.*

After class on Friday I asked a bunch of kids to stay behind. I kept Perry the longest. His flunking another quiz was of no interest to either of us. I said, 'I want us to stop.'

The light was grey. Someone had left behind a Grizzlies sweatshirt. It was puddled beneath a desk in the front row. I couldn't remember who'd been sitting there.

'It's okay,' he said. 'I've been feeling like you were going to say it for a long time.'

'Well, I haven't been comfortable with this for a long time. It was a bad idea for a lot of reasons. And I'm sorry I took it so far. I was the adult. I should have stopped it.'

'I'm not going to tell anyone,' he said, and laughed. 'You don't have to make me feel better.' But there was something brittle in the way that he said it. I felt new about him, somehow maternal and sad.

Still, though, I felt good when I drove home. Clean blood. I was certain of things. Lux told me about an article she'd read on memorial architecture. We cooked a complicated sort of a meal together, used the polenta we'd bought last time we were in Fresno. We had time for all that.

The phone rang when we were eating. It was Perry.

'I know I can't come over,' he said. 'I thought you might want to meet someplace else.'

'You're mistaken. You have the wrong number.'

'I just thought I'd ask,' he said, 'if you wanted to meet someplace else.'

'I don't,' I said.

There was a noise like a car starting up on his end. Boys' voices. Perry was speaking close to the receiver. His consonants made a soft thud in my ear.

In the other room, Lux was watching TV.

'Listen,' I said, 'I know I've made this difficult for you. I'm sorry about it.'

He said nothing. The noise on his end had died. I wondered if he'd gone someplace else. Then he said, 'We always did exactly what you wanted, Joanna.'

It was the first time he'd ever called me by my name.

I cleared my throat. 'I am sorry,' I said. 'This is a different number to the one you want.'

I went back to the fold-out, where I'd left my plate on a cushion beside Lux. We were watching something about the wirewalkers who crossed Niagara Falls. It was on the Nature Channel but

I couldn't see why. There was nothing natural about it.

The phone rang again. Lux looked at me. I set down my plate and went to the kitchen to answer it.

'*Hello?*'

'You okay? Christ, that was like gunfire.'

'Oh, Jeff,' I said. 'It's you.'

'Yes,' my brother said in a strange voice. I thought he was going to tell me some bad news then, but he only started to laugh. All the blood rushed to my ankles.

'You missed Maria,' Lux said when I sat down again. I felt as if I were looking at things underwater. 'Maria Spelterini,' she said. 'The first and only woman to cross the gorge on a tightrope.'

V

On Tuesday morning we had a staff briefing. A girl had been sexually assaulted, a sophomore. Kelly Murphy. I didn't know her.

Lynn, the social studies teacher, started to cry. 'That shouldn't have happened to any of our girls,' she said. 'One of our *own*.' The rest of us looked at one another, a little embarrassed.

Mike cleared his throat, picked up where he'd stopped talking. He was our assistant principal. He had a face like a losing politician's. 'Obviously, we need to be taking this very seriously. The assault took place on school grounds, and we need to make sure the students are supported and feeling safe. We also need to avoid, as far as possible, any sort of mass hysteria.'

I raised my hand. 'When will parents be informed?'

'We're still discussing that. We'll work on a letter this morning.' I stopped listening. I was thinking about the high school where

I'd taught in Crenshaw. Shit happened all the time, but there'd never been anything like this on campus.

I didn't mention it to Lux because she wasn't there when I got home. There was a note that said she'd gone out for coffee with one of the work girls before her shift started, and I thought that it was nice that she'd made a friend, since it didn't always come easy to her. I changed into my jeans and boots. I put on my rain jacket. I decided I'd walk to the creek. I rolled a cigarette to have halfway there. Kelly Murphy was a sophomore. Kelly Murphy was in Spanish Club. Kelly Murphy's yearbook picture said nothing. She wore a denim jacket. Her hair was flat and straight, the way all the girls wore theirs. Her brother was the District 6 Rough Stock Director of the California High School Rodeo Association. I didn't know her. I kept thinking about Lynn saying *one of our own*, as if there were an outfield of other children. Lux pronounced *creek* as *crick*. She said it was a northerneastern states thing, but I'd never known anyone to say it like that until I met her.

Kelly Murphy was in Spanish Club. Kelly Murphy was one of our own.

I didn't know I was crying until I went to light my cigarette and realised there was noise coming from me. It was dusk. I had a flashlight in one hand. It kept bumping against my thigh. In the morning Lux would examine the salvo of grey bruises there and ask what happened. I'd say, *I don't know, maybe it's from leaning against my desk when I'm teaching*, and not know why I was lying, and she'd say, *repeated-action bruises*, and touch them with her lips and ask if it hurt.

• • •

215

Back home I moved from room to room. I was useless. I didn't know what to do. My head was full with something I couldn't name, a dull metallic humming like the sound of the airplanes landing close by, so loud when we first moved to LA. I lay on the bed. I wanted to be unconscious, but the strongest thing we kept in the bathroom these days was melatonin, which, Lux liked to say, *does shit-fuck except make you feel like you're trying.* Eventually I got up and called her.

'Yosemite Gateway Inn, this is Lux. How may I help you?'

'Hi there, I was wondering if you still had any rooms available for this evening,' I said, trying for a thick Midwestern accent, a man's voice. Somehow she fell for it.

'Certainly, sir. Is it just yourself?'

'It's me and my girlfriend. You might know her—she's petite, really hot, tattoo of a Shel Silverstein drawing on her arm.'

She was laughing down the line. 'You fucking idiot,' she said. 'That voice was full-on *Fargo*. Don't ever use it again.'

'How's it going?'

'Slowly. I feel like I've been here a week.'

'Can I come up?'

I made a thermos of coffee to take. It was raining lightly. There was a restaurant attached to the lodge, but they closed early on weeknights, and Lux wasn't supposed to leave the desk. The restaurant was where we'd eaten when we came to check out our house, way back in the summer. It was packed then. We kept whispering *Oh my God* at the carved wooden bear, the gaudy lampshades and carpet, the paintings of galloping horses, the laminated menus with looped cursive and pictures of mountains. *This is it*, Lux had said. *This is the decider. We have to move here.*

I pulled into the lot and saw her waving at me from behind the desk. She was trapped in that golden-lit cubicle meant to welcome weary travellers. A rush of cold air followed me in. She stood and kissed me, went to find some mugs. The room keys with their heavy plastic keyrings hung from numbered hooks. I ran my finger along them and set them rippling. On the desk was a half-eaten sandwich, a glass of apple juice and a Leslie Marmon Silko novel I'd never read. Her internet browser was open to a page of documentaries on conspiracy theories.

'There were deer earlier,' she said, 'up by the playground.'

She'd grown up outside Syracuse, so I never really understood her enthusiasm for deer, but certain things were always remarkable to her.

Headlights outside: a car pulled into the lot beside mine. A man in a puffy jacket climbed out. I saw a woman yawn in the passenger seat, two children asleep open-mouthed in the back. Lux stood to greet him. A bright voice came out of her. *Absolutely, sir, the crib's already set up.* She chatted with him while she took his credit card, clicked around on the computer screen. *And do you have mud and snow tyres? They'll have the little letters on them? That's okay, you can check tomorrow. Why don't you just go on up and get some sleep now. They'll want to know you've got chains at the gate, but you can worry about all that tomorrow.* She reached for a key from the row of hooks, still trembling where I'd disturbed them. She pressed a map into his hand. They beamed at each other.

We watched him fold himself back into the car, hand the room key to the woman.

'M and S tyres,' I said, and we were both laughing.

'I know,' she said. 'I know. My dad would be so impressed.'

We fell quiet again.

'You okay, babe?' she asked after a while.

'I don't know,' I said. 'I cried this afternoon.'

She turned to me right away, put both hands on my knees.

'What happened? What's going on?'

'My head just feels so full, I can't stand it.'

'Tell me. Tell me what's the matter.'

'I don't know,' I said. I hated myself. It was such a bald lie that I started to cry again.

We went back to LA for our friends' engagement party. In the car we both said over and over again, *This is good, we needed this.* We camped in a tent in their backyard for the weekend. I got afternoon drunk and we escaped downtown. We walked all the way to Chinatown with nothing in mind. It was too cold for LA; it was all anyone talked about that weekend. The sky was white. We were both in our big coats. We held hands. We talked about everything and the world. We bought sticky coconut bread buns and ate them on the walk back. Lux stopped to hang her arms over the concrete railing above the Santa Ana freeway. She smiled at me, sleepily, where I stood. In one fist was the balled-up paper bag from the Chinese bakery. The wind was in the thin palms. It was in her yellow hair. Her arms were reaching for the overpass, as if she could pick up the I-5 and pour it down her throat.

'I never thought I'd miss this. I miss it like my mom,' Lux said. 'And I never thought I'd miss my parents.'

'There's nothing here,' I said. 'Big city.'

'Only for the weekend,' she said.

Walking back to the bus station she had her hand under my coat, in the back pocket of my jeans.

At Nate and Marta's all the cars were still parked out front, and we could hear them in the yard. We staggered down the drive, kissing and laughing. We kissed under the oleander. We told each other we tasted of coconut. The sky was almost dark. In the back-yard Nate said, *Where the fuck were you two, we missed you,* and hugged us both at once. We made pizza. We borrowed hats and scarves from Marta. Someone went to the store to get more tomato juice, and came back with a cat. Marta and Nate made a funny, clumsy speech. We all went for a midnight walk to the lumber yards. It felt good to be small again. There were no stars in the city.

All night Lux made cuba libres for other people, sliced limes the size of baseballs. She didn't drink any more, but she was gracious about it. I'd never once heard her say she wished she could join; that she missed it. After everyone had gone home I vomited on the avocado tree. Lux said, *Baby, you're so fucked up*, in a tone both gentle and disgusted. She hosed down the patch of soil where I'd been sick. She sang to me until I passed out.

We got the news only just before the kids did. There was another meeting. Afternoon, this time, the end of the day. There weren't enough seats. I stood at the back of the room, close to the door. There was a draught at my back. I didn't hear much of what Mike said past the first few sentences. My whole body was electric. Some hot doom had invaded me. It was in my guts, the tops of my thighs. I slipped out of the faculty room. I was in the parking lot shivering, fumbling for my keys, before I realised it was snowing. I'd left my coat inside. I drove home blindly. Half a mile from our house, I pulled over to the shoulder. I slid my hands beneath my thighs and sat on them. After five minutes I held them up. They'd stopped shaking. I looked at my eyes in the rear-view mirror. I flicked on the headlights and drove home.

Lux was cutting up vegetables in the kitchen. She was playing a Karen Dalton record, singing along. I dropped my bags on the floor, stood looking at her dumb.

'Is it still snowing?' she asked. She kissed me, her elbows either side of my face, holding her hands away from me. They smelled of onion.

I shook my head. 'I think it was just a dump. All at once, now nothing.'

'Some Mariposa High kid's been arrested for assault. Rape,' Lux said. 'You know him?'

'He's in my English class,' I said.

She turned back to the chopping board. 'Shit.'

'How'd you find out?'

'Annie. Her son's on the wrestling team with him. Apparently it was in a classroom. How the fuck does something like that happen?'

'Lux,' I said. 'I know you've just started dinner but do you— would you take me to the park?'

She turned around, looked right at me. 'The big one?'

'I've just had a motherfucker of a day,' I said, 'and I feel like being outside. And I don't want to drive. I wouldn't ask if I really didn't have to.'

'Okay. Of course,' she said. She was already washing her hands, already pulling on a sweater. She yelled, *Are you okay*, from the bedroom, and I said, *Yeah, it's just been a weird day*, and she emerged in a woolly hat, looking at me closely but still moving, still prepared to take me where I wanted. We didn't talk about it any more, just got into the car and drove the fifteen miles to the park entrance. Our annual pass dangled from the rear vision mirror. The guy at the gate asked us if we had chains. Pearly dusk skies. We drove down to the sequoia grove. We were the only ones in the parking lot. Lux pulled in by the shelter with its maps, its warnings about bears. The handbrake made a violent grating sound as she pulled it to. We sat in the half-dark, looking out at where the headlights threw their yellow glow. Lux cut the engine.

'This place is full of devils,' she said. I got out of the car. I started walking up the snowy slope. I tried to stick to the

ACKNOWLEDGMENTS

Several of the stories in this collection were originally published in Australian literary journals and magazines, including *Overland, Kill Your Darlings, Australian Book Review* and *Sleepers Almanac.* I'm overwhelmingly thankful to these publications, as well as countless others, which support and encourage short fiction—my favourite form, I think, but one not widely read in Australia. Thank you for making a space for it.

A few of these stories were conceived or written while I was undertaking a residency at Can Serrat in El Bruc, Catalonia, in 2015. The time I spent at there was the most productive and intensive period of my career to date. Montserrat truly did feel like a magic mountain to me, and I'm eternally grateful. *Moltes gràcies.*

I'm also indebted to the Wheeler Centre's Hot Desk Fellowship, of which I was a recipient in 2014, and to the Vermont Studio

Center, where I spent my residency redrafting, among others, the title story, in 2016. Both of these fellowships provided me with critical time, space and support to write.

Thank you, Tom Fairman, for helping me understand what constitutes the day-to-day of a forest scientist back in 2013. You somehow knew precisely the kind of detail I was after. Thank you, Robert Cohen, for suggesting the tweak that fixed 'Pulse Points'. It seemed like a small thing, but I'm very appreciative of your sharp eye and generosity as a reader.

Thank you, Danielle Dominguez, Sarah Craig and Amy Nicholls-Diver, for being the best colleagues and always encouraging me to keep working at my other job when I left the office.

Thank you, Melissa Manning, Thomas Minogue, Yasmine Sullivan and Kieran Stevenson, for your skill as writers and readers; your humour; your kindness. When I think of my tentative drafts, I always remember sitting around Yas's kitchen table and one of you going, *Oh, trees and a dog and a sad bloke with a floppy dick—Carrie'd love it*—and I knew, then, that the story might have legs after all.

Thank you, Laura Stortenbeker and Bec Varcoe, for keeping me sane in this weird writing world. I'm always in awe of both of you—your writing, your warmth, your patience—but most importantly, you both make me laugh in an ugly way (mostly over stuff at which I would otherwise despair) every single day.

I still can't believe how fortunate I am to work with Text. My gratitude in particular to Elena Gomez, for her poet's ear and deft editorial hand, and to Alaina Gougoulis, for seeing the shape of things. It's a privilege to entrust one's work to such wonderful editors. Thanks, too, to Imogen Stubbs for the beautiful cover, and to Michael Heyward for championing my work.

Finally, a reservoir of gratitude and love for Tasha, Kathleen, Bianca, Claire, Jasna, Steph, Lucas, Jonathan, Bridget and Liadan.

Thanks (or double thanks) to Tasha, Jasna, Jonathan and Aya for being dream cohabitants.

Thank you, family. Sophie and Lilly, I'm supposed to be older but I'm forever looking up to your compassion, wit and thoughtfulness. Thank you, Mama and Dad, for cheering us all on, no matter what we do. Thanks for reading to me. Thanks for tuning me to the frequency of other people's lives.